I0664303

SHATTER YOUR IMAGE

DEAR READER

We're so glad you're here. I'd like to take this opportunity to tell you a little more about Realize Your Beauty, and why this anthology is so important to us.

Realize Your Beauty is a not-for-profit organization that promotes positive body image to youth through theatre arts. We strive to educate adolescents about the dangers of dieting and disordered eating. We encourage students to love themselves, practice self-care, and learn the warning signs of an eating disorder.

Our workshops focus on fostering inner beauty—taking the focus away from societal standards and the pressure to be "pretty." We encourage students to put their energy into kindness, integrity, and respect towards themselves and others, and focus on developing their own unique inner qualities.

Some of you may be here because you yourself feel "not good enough," not worthy of self-love and self-care. To you I would like to say: we are most beautiful when we are the most ourselves. Everyone has unique gifts to offer the world. Whenever you're not feeling good enough, try to remember these qualities you have to offer. A great deal of self-love and acceptance comes from kindness. When we can learn to be kind to ourselves, we can learn to be kind to others. Through this kindness and self-love, we will see real change in this world.

Our beauty-obsessed culture creates an environment that is very damaging for young minds. Children grow up with negative messages surrounding them. They're constantly being told that they are somehow not good enough: they're not tall enough (or are too tall), they're not thin enough (or are too thin), their hair is too meager or too thick or the wrong texture or the wrong color, their nose is too big or too crooked or too small. The list goes on and on.

A world where children grow up feeling that there is something inherently wrong with them is a world where children do not grow up loving and respecting themselves. When a child does not love and respect themselves, they do not respect others. When a child is not kind to themselves, they are not kind to others.

We live in a world where too many children are taught that if they do not meet impossibly high standards of cultural beauty, they are worthless. They are not taught the value of developing their inner beauty. They are not taught integrity. Children are not taught to develop their own special and unique qualities, which make them their individual selves.

We believe it's time for CHANGE. We envision a different world where children are given a different message.

Imagine a young girl. She is given permission to accept herself. She learns from a young age to love herself. She is taught that there is nothing wrong with her—that she is good enough, just as she is. As this child grows to love herself, she learns to respect herself. She learns to be kind to herself. In turn, this child learns to be kind and respectful towards others.

One child after another growing with these values creates a generation of children who are kind and respectful of unique human qualities. We'd have a generation of children who grow up learning to develop these unique traits; a generation of children that feels empowered is a generation that will change the world.

These short stories encompass the voices of people from all parts of the world, who share this vision and goal.

Please enjoy this anthology.

Stacey Lorin Merkl
Founder & Executive Director, Realize Your Beauty

CONTENTS

ACKNOWLEDGMENTS

To tackle a subject like this took a lot of courage and sacrifice from a lot of people. Thank you to Kyla Umemoto for her patience and fantastic design, to Bree Crowder for meticulous copy-editing, and Melissa Koons for marvelous formatting. To the authors and poets, thank you for providing your work and honesty to this anthology. And also thank you to Realize Your Beauty, for providing a platform for this anthology to exist and coming along for this journey.

RAMSEY
Jessica Lauren Gabarron

Looking at my reflection wasn't one of my favorite things to do, especially when I was sharing a mirror with my best friend. Alannah snuck over to my house after her family drove her out late the night before. It wasn't an uncommon occurrence. She had a drawer of stuff in my dresser for exactly this reason.

She didn't even sleep in her own bed, and she still looks picture perffffect. The voice in my head was un-welcomed but not unexpected. *Look at the bagssss under your eyes, your greassssy hair. No one will ever notice you next to her.*

Alannah applied her make-up with a practiced hand, her long, thick blonde hair cascading in soft waves down her back. "Melissa, are you okay?" she asked.

I managed a smile. "Of course, just tired." Tired of feeling like I always lacked. My limbs felt heavy. I wanted coffee; I hoped it would alleviate my exhaustion.

Ramsey, the voice in my head, was right. Alannah had gotten up and showered, but I had tried to cling to the last bits of sleep I was going to get. Even after I finished curling my unwashed hair it fell lifeless to my shoulders. The make-up I'd once thought made my mud-brown eyes pop now just made me feel like I had two black eyes. I felt even frumpier and fatter walking next to Alannah, who carried herself with grace.

When we were ready, Alannah drove us to school.

"How do your parents never notice you sneaking out?" I asked. "It's not like you sneak off into the night like a ninja." The rumble of her old car was anything but stealthy.

"Like they notice anything," Alannah said. "I could probably have sex on the kitchen table during dinner and they'd just use it as something to fight about."

I knew the feeling.

Your father doesn't even want to sssstay in the same house as you. He'll be so glad when you leave. You're such a burden, Ramsey hissed.

At least my first class was biology. I saw an orca in real life at a theme park and I fell in love with the black and white beauty. I wanted to study the wolves of the sea and see the world. Science was one of the few classes I didn't struggle through. Biology came easy. Figuring out how it all worked made sense to me.

It's ssss too bad that you're not ssssmart enough to be a sssscientissssst.

I inwardly cringed at Ramsey's words.

Mr. Johnson handed out the lab we'd be working on for the next week: fetal pig dissection. Instead of letting us pick our own partners, he decided to add to the torture and pair us off. Not that it mattered much; I had no friends in this class.

"Melissa James and Dean Knight."

I cringed. Dean Knight? Really?

He'ssss going to laugh at you. He's going to know that you're sssstupid.

My hand tightened around my pen. Ramsey lived inside of me, lying in wait to remind me at every turn that I was worthless. Too fat. Too stupid. A joke for others to laugh at.

Maybe you should skip school tomorrow. Avoid making a bigger fffffool of yourself.

Ramsey's voice echoed my own fears. I squeezed my eyes shut, wishing that Ramsey would shut up. His hypnotic voice rang with truth; it was hard for me to fight him. And why should I? Ramsey was always right.

Mr. Johnson gave us the last five minutes of class to meet with our partners. A deep, baritone voice caught my attention. "Well, James, I guess you're stuck with me."

I strained my neck to meet his hazel eyes and wiped my clammy, trembling hands on my jeans. "How will I survive?" I said, managing a smile.

2

He chuckled, flipping his shaggy sun-kissed hair out of his eyes. "This'll be fun."

You're worthlessss. You can't even talk to the guy. He must think you're such a losssser.

"I call cutting out the brain," I said, laughing a little. My cheeks heated as I worried that he might think I'm weird or weirder than he already thought.

Relief flooded his face. "Oh, good. I wasn't sure I'd be able to stomach that."

"Really?"

"It's probably not manly, but I'm really not excited about cutting open a baby pig."

His confession made me like him a little more. "Don't worry, I'll make sure your reputation remains intact, Knight. I can do the slicing and dicing. If you'll look at my résumé, you'll see that I got an A on the frog dissection."

"You are quite the scientist." He winked at me. "You always were the best one."

My cheeks heated. I looked away, unsure of what to do with the compliment. Mostly, I figured he was just being nice. Thankfully, the bell rang. I quickly slid my stuff into my backpack, tossed it over my shoulder, and stood.

"Where you headed next?" Dean asked.

"Calculus."

"Mrs. Heath?"

I nodded. "Yeah. She's killer."

Don't you feel ffffat next to him? He couldn't even get his armssss around you.

Feeling extra stout next to Dean's long, lean form made me tug on the bottom of my shirt to make sure my bulbous stomach was covered. I glanced at his muscular arms peeking out of his t-shirt. I didn't want to walk next to him anymore.

I made a note to pop a couple extra diet pills before lunch. Softball try-outs were coming up. Fear paralyzed me in the years before. I never made it to the field, but I wanted to play.

No one wants to watch an elefffphant playing softball.

We reached my classroom. "I guess I'll see you later."

He flashed me another smile. "You bet. I'll see you in biology tomorrow. Have fun."

I scoffed. "Yeah, right." I watched him as he walked away. Was I imagining the look in his eye? Maybe he did like to spend time with me.

Definitely imagining. He wants nothing to do with you. He thinks you're a losssser.

I slumped into my desk near the front of the class, propping my head on my hand. Of course he wanted nothing to do with me. I was a fat cow. I couldn't even get my hair to curl nicely, and I was sure that even though it was only second period, my eye makeup was smudged, adding to my existing raccoon eyes. It baffled me that Dean even tolerated being seen with me.

*   *   *

By lunchtime, I felt like a beaten puppy (as usual). It had grown more difficult to fight Ramsey, and lately I was afraid that he was winning. I worried that I echoed him more than I argued with him.

Tucked in a dark corner of the cafeteria, far from most of the chatty popular kids, I scarfed down pizza, hoping that no one saw. Ramsey had pointed out that "thin" wasn't an obtainable goal, and pizza was much more delicious than salad. I got the greasy, fatty option, not caring if it ended up on my fat thighs. I didn't care that I was secluded. Ramsey was easier to deal with if no one was around. Or maybe it just felt easier.

"Mel!"

I looked up to find Alannah bouncing toward me. Just before she reached the table, she wiggled her hips and shimmied her chest. The snickers from nearby tables didn't even faze her. I smiled as she danced into her seat across from me. "How's it going?" she asked.

"Okay. We're doing the pig dissection tomorrow and I have to do it with Dean Knight."

Alannah's face lit up. "That's exciting."

I dropped my head into my hand. "I think the word you're looking for is 'devastating.'"

"Ah, come on, Mel. Dean's awesome. I think you kind of like him." She waggled her eyebrows at me, grinning.

4

Alannah probably likessss Dean. He'll never noticccce you next to her. He'll never noticcccce you at all.

I cringed. Ramsey was right. Alannah was beautiful and adventurous. She talked to everyone, and everyone remembered her. No one ever remembered me. I didn't even know why Alannah hung out with me.

She's ussssing you. Alannah doesn't need you, but you do everything she wantssss.

"I do not like Dean," I grumbled.

"Uh, yeah, you do. Deny it all you want, but I've seen the way you look at him. And I think he likes you too, but you're always so… quiet."

"I'm quiet?" I snarled.

No one lissssstenssss to you. No one hearssss you. No one caressss.

"It's not like anyone cares what I have to say anyway." I took a deep breath, trying to take the edge out of my voice.

"Mel, don't say that. You're the smartest person I know," she said.

I looked up at her. "Oh come on, Alannah, you know that I'm invisible. No one but you gives a crap about me. Honestly, I don't even know why you want to be around me. Even my own dad wants nothing to do with me."

Alannah sat back. I could see the hurt in her eyes. "It's Ramsey, isn't it?"

I sighed. "What does it matter?"

"It does matter. You've gotten worse. I feel like you're not able to hold him back anymore. Can't we figure out a way to get rid of him?"

I shrugged, sure there was no way. "I don't even know… *what* he is."

Alannah leaned back. Her eyes narrowed as if she was trying to see inside me. "We should figure it out. And get rid of him."

My brow furrowed. "What? Like an exorcism?"

She leaned forward, resting her arms on the table. "Maybe. If that's what it takes."

"I'm pretty sure people have died from exorcisms."

"Not an actual exorcism. We need to figure out what Ramsey is first."

I frowned. "You're serious."

"Mel, I've watched Ramsey beat you down, talk you out of things. You didn't join the school newspaper. You wouldn't turn in your story in creative writing. You won't do anything that means putting yourself out there. Standing out. Shining. Mel, you should shine."

She just wants to outsssshine you. And it's sssso easy for her.

"I'm not amazing."

Alannah sighed. "Are you going to try out for softball?"

"Yes," I said, "of course I am." The notion terrified me. I loved sports as much as I loved writing, but I knew I was setting myself up to fail. Who would want a fat, out of shape, useless waste of space on their team?

Loserssss.

Alannah's eyes narrowed as if she could see the doubt swimming beneath the surface. "Well, I'll be there for you, cheering in the stands."

"Oh, please don't do that. I just want to get through it, count it as a failure, and go on with my life."

"It's not going to be that bad. I've seen you play. You're good."

I squirmed in my seat. Compliments always felt wrong, like lies. "My dad still hasn't said whether he can afford to get me a glove or anything."

"I've got some money saved up. We'll get you what you need."

"Alannah, you don't have—"

"Shhh, nonsense. I want to help you. You always help me."

You're not worth it. She shouldn't wasssste her time or money helping you.

I packed up my stuff. "I should get going." I didn't want to give Ramsey any more reasons to talk. "See you after school."

"I'm serious about Ramsey. You don't need to deal with him alone. We can figure out something."

I managed a weak smile before I ran off. I didn't want to start crying. The louder Alannah got, the more Ramsey chimed in with the truth.

*   *   *

Once I got home, I found a note from my dad saying that he would be with his boyfriend again. I turned on the television, trying to drown out the suffocating silence. I milled around eating junk food, rummaging through movies and books, trying to keep myself distracted. The ringing phone interrupted my pity party.

"You wanna come over? Watch a movie or something?" Alannah asked.

"I should study," I lied. I wanted nothing more than to curl up on the couch alone.

"All right. Call me if you need anything."

I threw my phone onto the far end of the couch. Why didn't she know something was wrong?

She doesn't care, just like your father doesn't care. Your mother certainly didn't.

I always wondered if my mother would be proud of me or disappointed. I felt like I never had the typical mother/daughter relationship with her. She was always distant, not very affectionate, but she and I laughed a lot over ridiculous inside jokes. Dad always told me that I laughed like her.

I got up from the couch and opened the closet that had the last remnants of my mother's belongings. I pulled out a box with pictures inside.

She died when I was eight years old. There were only a few photos of us together at all. Rummaging through the box, I came across something else: a journal tied with leather straps. I vaguely remembered my mother scribbling in it.

I untied the bindings. The pages crackled as I pulled the book open. The entries weren't dated. I traced the loops and curves of the words. The more I read, the more my heart sank.

Was my mother infected with something like Ramsey? Her words mimicked my own journal entries. Perhaps it was more accurate to say that my words echoed hers. She talked about her own shortcomings like they were truths, but everyone loved my mom. I knew that she worked hard through college. She found a man to treat her well after she divorced my dad. Seeing the same self-doubt and self-hate was shocking. Some of the phrases were almost word-for-word in my journal.

How could this be possible? How did I not know my own mom was in so much pain?

Your mother couldn't find her way out of the darknessssss and neither will you.

I slammed the journal closed, but took it with me. Breathless, I picked up my phone. "Yo, homeslice," Alannah said.

"Hey. What are you up to?"

"Killing my brother on his own Xbox. You?"

"I want to figure out what Ramsey is," I said. "I want to destroy him."

There was a moment of silence. "I'll be right over."

I sat on the couch with my mother's journal as I waited for Alannah. What was I doing?

You can never desssstroy me. You belong to me. No one will ever love you. You're worthlessssss.

I squeezed my eyes closed, trying to shut out his deep voice, counting down the seconds until Alannah arrived. Finally, I heard her car pull up. I jumped off the couch, not waiting for her to ring the bell. Once Alannah was inside, we sat at the kitchen table and got out our laptops.

I sighed. "What exactly are we looking for?"

Alannah also sighed. "I'm not sure. What brought all this on?"

I set my mother's journal on the table. "Maybe it's nothing, but I think my mom was infected with something like Ramsey."

Her brow furrowed as she looked at the journal. "Why?"

"Her journal entries could be my own. I think this all started with her. Whatever infected her is in me now."

Your mother didn't love you. Why would she give you anything? She wouldn't even sssshare me.

I cringed as Ramsey hissed. I rubbed my eyes, trying to keep my focus.

"All right. That gives us something to start looking for."

After hours of searching the internet, Alannah perked up. "Here's something."

I looked up from my computer. "Whatcha got?"

"Daemonum Interius," she said with confidence.

I frowned. "What is that?"

"There's all kinds of them. They get inside people with weaknesses they're attracted to. They make them think or do all kinds of horrible things, usually capitalizing on those initial weaknesses."

"Like what?"

"Murder people. Bully people. There are some that…" she trailed off.

"That what?"

She shifted uncomfortably. "That make their hosts commit suicide."

Tears instantly burned my eyes. Did my mother really have something like this inside of her, rotting her brain?

Alannah moved around the table and pulled me into her arms. She held me for a while as I cried, stroking my hair and telling me everything would be okay. I couldn't see how; everything felt awful. Why was my mother infected with something like Ramsey? Why did she deserve such a terrible fate?

"Does it say how you get rid of them?"

"There're a few different theories," Alannah said quietly.

"Like what?"

"They're kind of out there," she said. "It sounds like magic."

I pulled on the rubber bracelet around my wrist, staring blanking into the wood grain of the table. "I have to get rid of him." My voice felt barely audible, but I kept going. "I don't want to keep going down this road. Something has to change. Every day he gets stronger. I don't want to fight myself and him." I wiped away a few stray tears. "That's what it feels like every time I get out of bed instead of just staying buried under the blankets."

Alannah blinked at me. "Why didn't you tell me that it was getting this bad?"

I shook my head. "He's winning. I try to put on a brave face, but it takes all my energy just to keep moving forward."

"All right, then we're going to stop him."

I nodded. "How do we do it?"

"There's some pretty creepy stuff in here, and the ingredients list is disgusting. Also, you have to give up blood. I just… I don't know, Mel. This is scary stuff."

"It's a lot scarier in my head."

Alannah frowned. "What is he saying?"

"It's not important, but it makes it hard to keep functioning." I didn't want to say the words out loud. I didn't want to give him a voice outside of myself. Tears filled my eyes again.

Alannah put her hand over mine. "Okay, we don't have to talk about it."

"I just… I don't want to say it out loud."

Alannah moved back to her computer. "There are a few different testimonials here on how to get rid of them. It sort of sounds like a spell or something. I'm not sure where we're going to get some of this stuff, but we'll find it. In the meantime, you've got to stay strong. Maybe I should stay with you until we get rid of this thing?"

I shook my head. "That's ridiculous. I'll be okay."

Alannah checked her phone for the time. "I should probably get home. We'll start tracking down this stuff tomorrow. I know of a couple of New Age-y places that might have what we're looking for."

Once Alannah left, I felt the dangerous silence again. I turned on the television, but Ramsey was there.

Your friend can't help you. You've chassssed away most of your friends. You'll chasssse her away too. She can't sssstop me, and you certainly can't sssstop me. You can't sssstop what's happening to you. You're mine. You belong to me.

"Shut up," I said out loud.

You have no power over me. You're mine fffforever.

"I have power over me." I stood.

Ramsey growled in my head; the vibrations echoed outside of my head. The DVDs on the shelf shook as the lights flickered. I covered my ears and closed my eyes.

You are nothing. You are unloved. No one wantssss you. You're sssstupid. FFFFat. Ugly. There is nothing worthwhile about you and there never will be.

His voice thundered in my head. It hurt. I covered my ears in vain. Now that I was engulfed in darkness, I felt defenseless.

Someone could break in and tear you limb from limb and no one would know for dayssss. Your father doesn't care. He won't check in on you. Your mother wanted to get away from you so badly she wouldn't let you ssssee her in the hospital. The cancccccer wouldn't kill her fast enough, so she killed herself just to get away from you. No one caressss about you. You would do the world a favor if you stopped exissssting. Just get a knife from the kitchen and end it. That'ssss the only way you'll ssssstop me.

I swallowed hard, tears streaming down my face. I often felt like everything would be better if I just ended it. I didn't want to be a burden. I didn't want to be such a waste of space.

Go to the kitchen, Melissssa. Do everyone a favor.

I screamed. I didn't know what else to do. My throat hurt as I cried out. Nausea swam in my gut. I charged through my house to get to my room. I grabbed the stuffed platypus that belonged to my mom, curled up on my bed, and pulled the blankets over my head. Ramsey didn't stop, but I fought the dark urges that Ramsey insisted on.

*　　　　*　　　　*

Biology class buzzed with chatter. The stench of formaldehyde drifted around the room.

"Everyone, get with your partner," Mr. Johnson said.

Sit at the end of the table. You don't want your ffffat to touch him. He's not going to want to sit close to you. He doesn't want your bloated, dissssgusting body near him.

Dean got our pig while I glanced over the work packet, deciding what needed to be done first. I considered my options. Did I listen to Ramsey, to my own fears? This was a partners' project but I didn't want him to feel like I was crowding him.

Feeling nauseated, I didn't rearrange the desk setup even though Ramsey kept hissing. Dean could see my big fat body. If he didn't want to be close to me, he could move.

Anger clouded my head. I felt angry at Dean too. Why did he have to be my partner? Why couldn't he just do the teenage eye roll, groan, and beg for a different partner?

Dean returned with the pan of not-so-fresh fetal pig and slipped into the chair next to me. He bumped my elbow and I instantly cringed. I flipped open the packet and immediately went to work, trying to keep my thoughts occupied.

"You're quiet today," Dean said.

I managed a weak smile. "I didn't sleep well."

"Everything okay?" he asked.

I shrugged. "You ever find something out about your history that sort of blows up your view of how things are now?"

He frowned. "I haven't, but that sounds pretty heavy. Do you want to talk about it?"

"Nah, I just… it just affected my sleep last night."

He nodded. "Well, I'm here if you ever want to talk."

He doesn't want to lissssten to you whine like a little baby. He doesn't really care. He wishessss you would just sssshut up.

I forced a smile despite Ramsey's words. "Thanks, Dean. I appreciate it."

"Any time. I mean that."

I smiled.

"Hey, didn't you tell me a while back that you were trying out for softball this season?"

My stomach sank. Why did he remember that? And worse, why didn't I remember that? "Softball try-outs are today," I said glumly.

"Uh, yeah, did you forget?"

I covered my face with my hands. "I did." Why couldn't they be a few days away, after we figured out how to deal with Ramsey? I didn't want him growling things while I tried to concentrate on the game.

I'll alwaysss be here.

"You're going to be great," Dean said. "I have no doubt. You were amazing in gym last year."

I blushed. "That was gym class. It's not like…"

"You're good, Melissa," he said earnestly.

"Thanks, Dean. I appreciate it. Hopefully my lack of sleep won't hinder me too much."

That won't be the only thing hindering you. You don't have any sssskill. You're not athletic. No coach would want a player like you. Ffffat and uselessss.

I sighed, looking determinedly at our fetal pig. Picking up the scalpel, I dissected it, imagining the scalpel cutting into Ramsey.

*   *   *

Nerves nearly incapacitated me as I stood at the edge of the softball field. I hadn't managed to get much down at lunch, and I felt queasy. Ramsey had deterred me from living my life for long enough. I didn't want to lose this chance. I grabbed one of the gloves that the coach provided and ran out onto the field.

I started in the outfield, but I kept eyeing second base. It's where I wanted to be. I heard the crack of the ball hitting the bat. It soared toward center field. I kept my eye on it as my feet started moving. I stretched my arm. The ball tapped against the end of my glove and hit the grass. My stomach sank, but I kept moving. My fingers wrapped around the ball and I twisted, and threw it to second base. The baseman caught it and the runner was out.

My breath was a little ragged, but I slowed myself and took a couple of deep breaths as the next batter went to base.

Ramsey barked out things as loud as he could, but I couldn't hear him over my own heartbeat. I listened to my heart, telling myself over and over that I could do this. Ramsey wasn't in control of me.

Coach kept shifting us on the field, testing our skill in each position. When the ball came my way again, I was on second base. I caught it and threw it to the first baseman's glove perfectly.

When it was my turn at bat, I swung as hard as I could. The crack and the vibrations from the bat hitting the ball startled me. I took off running for first base. The ball went flying into left field over the short stop's head, but landed in the grass before the left fielder could reach it. I ran as hard as I could. I got to second base.

Catching my breath, Ramsey slithered to the forefront. *You're out of sssshape. You're running like a hippo. The coach is already crosssssing you off her lisssst. Sssshe doesn't want you.*

My breath stalled in my chest. I squeezed my eyes shut, willing Ramsey to silence. I focused on the coach and her directions. We ran exercises, drills, and did more batting. As long as I focused on the present, Ramsey remained stifled by my determination.

Try-outs continued long into the afternoon. I was hot and sweaty by the time it was all over, but Ramsey wasn't talking to me. I felt good about what I'd accomplished. No matter the outcome, I'd done my best.

Alannah waited for me by the bleachers. "You looked great out there." She wrapped her arms around me.

"Well, thanks to you for helping me get into better shape," I said.

Alannah smiled. "Any time. It's not like you don't help me rehearse my lines."

I chuckled. "I made an awesome Claudio."

Alannah gave my shoulders a squeeze. "When will you know?"

"She's posting the team tomorrow."

Alannah nodded. "To distract you, we're going to get rid of Ramsey."

I was surprised when he didn't say anything.

"Let's do it."

*   *   *

"Is your dad ever home?"

"Not with the new boyfriend," I said. "I'm glad he's happy, but it would be nice to feel like I mattered to him too."

Alannah sighed. "I guess we're never happy with our situations. I would give anything for my parents to be gone all the time."

"Your parents suck. They're constantly riding you," I replied.

Alannah dumped all the ingredients into the middle of the floor. "Well, soon enough I'll be off to college and I won't have to listen to them anymore."

I picked up one of the jars full of pickled chicken feet. "Cheers to freedom."

Alannah made a face. "I'm just glad that you don't have to eat or drink any of this."

"What do we have to do?"

"We're calling the Daemonum Interius forward, into a shape or form that we can destroy."

"How exactly are we supposed to that?"

"That's the part that isn't clear," she said. "Sounds like it's different for every situation. Supposedly it's intuitive."

"Does it say how these things get inside of you in the first place?" I asked.

"It's all theories, but there's talk that they can be genetically handed down. You get them from your infected parents or guardians, or you're open to certain possessions because of traumas that happen to you. They feed on your insecurities or weaknesses. The Daemonum make them worse or more palpable. They try to make you only your weaknesses."

I knelt in front of Alannah. "What do I do?"

We slowly mixed together all of the ingredients, following the instructions perfectly. I kept waiting for Ramsey to make an appearance, to try to stop me.

"Ramsey's being uncomfortably quiet," I muttered.

"Maybe he's scared. You shined today, Mel. I've never seen you so fearless. Maybe it's affecting him too."

I knew better than to believe Ramsey was gone. Maybe he was trying to fool me into thinking I'd chased him away. "He's still here," I murmured. "I know he is."

Alannah sat back on her heels. "The final ingredient is a drop of your blood."

I wrinkled my nose and my lip curled up. I took the knife Alannah offered me. I summoned my courage, knowing the prick would hurt. I gently pushed the pointy tip into my finger. I jerked from my own assault. A droplet of blood pooled on my middle finger. I held it over the bowl. Once the blood hit the contents, the lights flickered and went out, leaving only the four candles we'd lit to represent North, East, South, and West.

Alannah looked around. "Well, that's not okay."

My mouth went dry. The dull ache in the center of my chest grew, as did my core temperature. The heat radiated into my limbs. "He's here. I can feel him." All the rot and illness that Ramsey constantly fed me now left a stench in the air like a rotting carcass. I stood up. "Don't leave this circle," I said. I was sure it was safe. Ramsey would've come for us already.

"Melissssa."

I shivered at the sound of Ramsey's discordant voice coming from the kitchen.

"Oh god, Mel."

"It's okay. I'm going to take care of him." I looked at the invisible barrier of the circle Alannah and I had created; I took a deep breath and stepped through it.

I heard Alannah shift. I wondered if she'd tried to stop me. It was too late now. I moved toward Ramsey.

Just before I reached the kitchen, a shadow appeared in the doorway. I couldn't make out any defining features at first. It was a round, fat figure, his shoulders visibly moving up and down with his ragged breath. "Ramsey," I said.

"Hello, Melisssssa," he hissed. "We meet at lasssst."

"This ends tonight," I said.

He shook his head slowly. "You don't have what it takessss to end me. Your mother certainly didn't."

My fists clenched at my sides. "You didn't know anything about my mother," I growled.

"Sssshe was weak. She didn't ffffight for herself, and she certainly didn't ffffight for you."

I took a step toward him. "She wasn't weak. She did the best that she could."

Ramsey jerked forward into the living room, causing me to trip backwards over my own feet. My breath caught when I saw him in the candlelight. I heard Alannah gasp as I scrambled further away.

He looked like me. Or at least how I pictured myself on my worst days—fat bubbling out from under my clothes, dark brown hair greasy and stringy with no real depth of color, and acne spread across his face like the plague. Crooked teeth gleamed at me through their yellow stains. He lumbered forward again, reminding me of the Stay Puft Marshmallow Man.

I curled my lip at the horrible vision. "You're not me," I yelled.

"I am what you see when you look in the mirror," he hissed. "The truth."

Alannah stood inside the circle with her arms wrapped around herself. Her eyes were crowded with worry and tears.

"Self-doubt is one thing, but you are evil."

"Is it evil to tell the truth?" Ramsey asked.

"I am loved." Nausea punished my gut, but I kept my chin high.

"Loved? Really? They'll all leave you in the dust and forget about you."

My face grew hotter as I clenched my fists, wanting to hit something, wanting to punch Ramsey. "I am more than capable of living my life."

"What liffffe?" he sneered.

"I am…"

Ramsey threw his head back and laughed. "You are worthlessssss."

The guttural scream bubbled up from the anguish and rage I buried deep inside of me. The dam burst and all of the fire I'd tried to smother over the years fueled me. I charged him.

"Mel!" Alannah cried out as I collided with Ramsey. It felt like I hit a concrete slab. He grabbed me by the neck, choking the breath out of me as he slammed me into the wall. My hands wrapped around his wrists as I tried to pull out of his grip. I flailed under his unrelenting hold on me. I tried not to look directly into his face. I didn't like seeing the distorted image of me. He was hideous.

His hand squeezed tighter. "Why couldn't you just be a good girl and kill yoursssself?" he snarled. "You're nothing."

As I stared into his bloated face, something shifted. I had my dad's oval eyes, but Ramsey's eyes were sad, more like my mother's.

"You tortured her," I choked out.

Ramsey's smile twisted into a toothy, malicious, almost maniacal grin. "Your mother was almost too easssssy. Everything that had been done to her… she already believed she was worthlessss."

Hot tears streamed down my cheeks. I remembered the sad look in my mother's eyes. She never found peace with herself. This demon was to blame.

"She tasted delicioussss. Ripe with self-loathing."

All the anger simmered and boiled up in my chest until I couldn't hold it in any longer. I pulled my leg back—like cocking a gun—and released the trigger. I kicked, clawed, and punched. Ramsey cringed. His grip loosened on my neck. I shoved him away. I gasped loudly as oxygen filled my starving lungs. Black dots filled my vision but I kept moving, trying to gain some distance and looking around for a weapon. "There was nothing wrong with her. You lied to her," I snarled.

Ramsey chuckled. "It was the truth to her, and it is the truth to you."

"No."

"Oh, yessss."

Tears streamed down my hot face. The ache in my chest only grew. I'd given him more power making him corporeal. I couldn't defeat him inside of me, what made me think I could defeat him at all?

"I loved my mom." My voice sounded small. "She did the best she could with what she had. If she was fighting you at the same time, then she's stronger than anyone I've ever met."

"Not as strong as you." Alannah's voice startled me. She held a candle and stood in the doorway behind Ramsey. "I've watched you fight Ramsey since the day I met you. I know you don't see it, but you shine anyway."

Ramsey laughed. "She shinessss with sweat from her gross, ffffat body. She's out of sssshape." He wheeled around to stare at me. "You're not going to make the softball team. You're not going to impress Dean Knight. There is nothing sssspecial about you. Your ffffriend will leave you too, when she sees you're too weak to defeat me."

Ramsey knocked the candle out of Alannah's hand and she stumbled backwards.

Ramsey kept moving after her. "Ramsey!" I cried, running toward them. I collided with him and we both hit the floor. We rolled across the living room, tangled together.

Ramsey thrust his elbow into my nose. Branches of sharp pain shot through my face. I stumbled backwards.

Ramsey turned back to Alannah. She crab-walked backwards as he went after her. "Get away from me!" she cried.

Ramsey's club fingers reached for Alannah. My head felt like it was being cooked, the hole in my chest growing wider. This was my fault. We'd brought this beast out into the real world thinking we could destroy it. Who knew what kind of havoc it could wreak? It was all my fault, and now he was going to win.

Ramsey's hands wrapped around Alannah's throat. She fought him the best she could, kicking and screaming against his grip. He turned to me; his skin looked like it was peeling away. His brown eyes were covered in a filmy white. "Once I've taken hold of her, you'll never know if what she's ssssaying is me... or her."

My eyes widened. I shook my head slowly at first, trying to deny the words. He couldn't do that. He wouldn't do that. Alannah's light was too bright to be extinguished by something like Ramsey. He couldn't do it.

I wouldn't allow it.

I pushed myself to my feet. I reached them, grabbing him by the collar. As I yanked him up I headed for the front door. "Get out!" We stumbled through the threshold together. "You have no power here. I will not listen to you. You can whisper in my ear all you want, but you're nothing. You'll starve to death with me. You're the past. I refuse to choke on you anymore."

Ramsey felt less like steel in my grip as I pushed him toward the stairs of the porch, trying to get him out of my house.

"I am strong. My mom might've given up. She might've had a hard time fighting after 40 years of you buzzing in her ear, but it ends with me. You can't be in my house, in my head. I won't let you near anyone I love."

I gasped when Ramsey started to melt. Skin oozed away from his face and he didn't resemble me or my mom anymore. Chunks of brown hair fell to the ground, along with clumps of skin.

"I will always fight. Always."

I jerked my hands away from Ramsey and shuffled back, not wanting to get any goo on me. Ramsey shrieked as the last of him fell away in a puddle of gross. The cool night wind gusted over the porch. Ramsey's shell turned to ash and blew away into the night. I sagged against the house, catching my breath. I wasn't even sure I really understood what had happened, but I felt lighter. I charged back into the house. "Alannah?"

"I'm here. Where is he?" She held a large knife.

I gave her a shakey smile. "I think he's gone."

Alannah's armed hand dropped. "Really?"

"I think so." I closed my eyes listening for him. It was only me left inside.

Alannah smiled. She dropped the knife and pulled me into a hug. "I had no idea what you were dealing with. He was so awful."

I hugged her back. "Thank you for giving me the strength I needed to get rid of him."

Alannah shook her head. "I didn't give you anything. You always had that strength."

We cleaned up the mess. We fixed the breaker and kept the lights on all night. Ramsey was gone, but the light helped us feel safe as we went to sleep.

*　　　　　*　　　　　*

Alannah and I didn't talk about it for a couple of weeks. We slept with night-lights and kept each other company. The more distance we put between us and the battle of Ramsey, the more things normalized. My head stayed clear and only my own doubts fluttered around.

Alannah drove us to school like always. "How do you think your mom got infected in the first place?" she asked as we parked one morning.

I pulled my gaze from the kids walking toward school. I blinked a couple of times as her words sank in. "I don't know," I said at last. "But if I had to guess, I would say she got it from her father, or maybe both her parents. I'm starting to think that insecurities are passed down. We pick up our cues from our parents about religion, politics... that's where it all starts, right? Why wouldn't self-esteem be part of that too?"

"I see your point. Are we all doomed?"

I chuckled. "No. We just can't let it get the better of us. We can't let it control us. Especially not fear. At least that's what I keep telling myself. I definitely still feel scared."

"Are you sure he's gone?" she asked.

"I think so." I shrugged. "It's hard to fight your own insecurities. Even if Ramsey is gone, I still have my own fears buzzing around up there."

"It was all for nothing?"

I shook my head. "I can't explain it, but knowing that my mom felt the way I did, I'm going to make myself try new things. Learn to be adventurous instead of hiding away. I killed Ramsey. It didn't turn the world on its axis, but it's one less thing that has power over me. I have power over myself again. That changes everything for me."

School didn't feel as intimidating. I kept my chin a little higher. I met people's gazes and smiled at them. I had the right to be there, sharing the space as much as anyone. When I got to biology, Dean smiled at me. I knew I wasn't imagining his smile or the glint of flirtation in his eyes. We also got an A on our pig dissection.

That afternoon, I stood in the dugout getting ready for my first softball game.

"Hey, Mel!"

I turned to find Alannah and Dean standing on the other side of the chain-link fence.

I grinned. "Hey!"

"We wanted to wish you luck," Alannah said.

"I'm glad you guys are here," I said.

"We'll be embarrassingly loud in the stands for you," Dean said.

I chuckled. "That's good. My dad said he would come."

"I'll keep an eye out for him," Alannah said.

I nodded. "Thanks." Nerves jumped around in my stomach, but there was excitement too.

"We'll celebrate after the game." Alannah nudged Dean toward the stands.

My newly oiled glove fit well; I looked forward to breaking it in. When the coach ordered us on the field, I ran across the diamond to my position at second base while my friends cheered for me from the stands. Murmurs of fears chattered in the back of my mind. Even when self-doubt crept back in now and again, I remembered my battle against Ramsey. Big moments were hard and scary; that's what life is.

The batter came out of the dugout and took her place at the plate. A smile curved my lips as I stared down my opponent; a loud crack hung in the air. The ball went up and I jumped. As I snatched away her chance to take first base, my grin grew wider.

Win or lose, I was going to shine.

DELETE DELETE
Aylâ Larsen

delete delete

We're taught delete delete.
That we are beautiful by elimination.

Ew, you have spider veins? OMG, sorry, but like gross…

Trim your waistline.
Remove your unsightly hair.
Get rid of your underarm sweat.

Why do you wear those lesbian shoes all the time?

Come on ladies,
help the world forget we are human!

So, I just started this new diet. You've tried it? Yeah, it's
hard without dairy.

I won't say we're beautiful anyway.
Because the word beautiful is tainted.
And it reinforces that being beautiful
should still be our primary goal in life.

Oh that bitch is crazy, but she's hot, so who cares?

I'll say this instead.

That we do not have to be all things.

So, do you miss your children while you're working?

Trim your shoulds.
Remove your guilt.
Get rid of your shame.

Come on girls, give us a smile.

delete delete delete delete delete delete delete delete delete

FIERCE THIS HOUSE
Caroline Rothstein

I will be bigger than heartbreak
I will be stronger than the empty choking guzzling in my
chest
I have sat alone at the largest canyon edge in Southeast
Utah and felt infinite
So, I will not be afraid

I will love this love's extinction into the depths of the
universe
I will scout my own way

I will birth this gully in my throat into a thousand
redemption songs and
I will bleed light from the contours of my eyes
I will march
I will march
I will march
I will eulogize every now abandoned kiss with
the sanctity of a marriage that will never be

I will sit this shiva
I will grieve this death
I will let my spirit stumble
I will rise again from breath

I will prevail
my heart will gift a thousand doves

to the outskirts of the universe
and I will call this freedom
I will call this love

I will hold myself
through every shiver
in the bathtub
in the shower
on my side of the bed
on the subway platform
on the phone with Chloe
in the car with my sister
on the curb of 14th Street and Avenue B
I will weep myself into tranquility
I will bless my goddess self
I will rise from this unshod journey
of what might otherwise become my blistered feet
my feet are massive
my feet are planted in the ground
I will not walk across the desert
I will lift into the clouds
I will stretch the tongue that used to kiss him
and thrust it with the fervor of a thousand ancient echoes
chanting to the full moon
I will be the full moon
I will light the sky
I will not hold back
I will not silence myself
I will not acquiesce

I will gift myself survival
and look back one day and know
I never even questioned
if I would come out complete

I will plant this foundation
I will fierce this house
I will burst this roof

I am not afraid to crumble
and if I cannot keep my words sacred
I will forgive myself
for I am no saint

but I will be my own savior
I will carry my whole breath
I will rise into the sunset
I will, empowered, resurrect

UNLEASHED
Beverly Coutts

The mirror girl's nude lip gloss,
plain fawn sweater, and prim ponytail
defined her as the perfect child,
a notched ruler to measure all others
and find them faulty.

Her lips parted in a disgusted sigh
that held no breath as she
shucked her sweater, discarded
skin coiled on the floor.

Her mother had called the lacy black bra
naughty as they passed it in the mall.
She wriggled into an emerald green tank top
and stretched like a newly shed reptile
to determine the capacity of her own skin.

Was that the shadow of the mirror girl's breast
or was her bra visible through the fabric?
She slicked her lips with a hue redder than the slap
her mother would deliver if she caught her.

Bold eyeshadow rivaled the green of her shirt
and she gilded her lashes like golden scales.
She shook her thick hair free of its confines,
tossed her head, and became a dragon
whose roar was trapped behind the glass.

The girl hefted her brush and hurled it
against the mirror with anger born of
years spent being told exactly who to be.
Shards fell and unleashed the mirror girl.

ANSWERING THE BELL
Jason Evans

Bess threw everything she had into that punch. Sweat, rage, fear and exhaustion. Then she threw another punch.

"Come on, princess. HARDER."

She could barely hear the voice, but she'd recognize her trainer anywhere.

"Faster, Bess. FASTER."

Jab. Jab. Jab. Cross. Jab. Hook.

"TIME."

Bess stepped away from the punching bag, drenched in sweat, sucking in air through her nose.

Her coach patted her on the back. "Alright, Bess, hit the showers."

Bess nodded, too tired to say anything, and walked into the locker room.

The shower felt amazing. The hot water soothed aching muscles while her troubles washed down the drain—if only for a moment. Bess couldn't linger too long though, as Mom needed help.

"Tomorrow, same time?" asked her trainer.

"Yep," Bess said as she walked out of the gym.

She walked the same route home through the same old neighborhood she always walked. Three blocks north, then the bus to the house.

"Stop!"

Bess turned to look in an alley.

"Give it up," someone said, and then came a crash.

Bess walked towards the commotion. Behind a stand of galvanized steel trash cans, two boys held and beat another boy, some three years younger.

"Hey, leave him alone!"

The two turned to look at her, then ran. Over the sounds of city traffic came the sounds of whimpering.

"Are you OK?" Bess asked.

The little boy said nothing while he sat in the alley and cried.

Bess looked in either direction, sighed, and scratched her nose. "Look, I gotta go, OK?"

The little boy's sobs didn't stop or slow down.

"Hey kid, you gotta stand up for yourself." Bess bent over to see the kid's face. He had a bruise over his left eye that was small, but growing. "Wow, that's a beauty."

"I couldn't get away," the boy explained between sobs.

"Come on, kid. Where do you live?" Bess started to dust the little boy off and help him to his feet. The boy pointed down the alley where Bess had come from. "Come on, kid, let's go."

Bess walked the little boy down to his bus stop. By the time the bus came, he'd stopped crying. The doors opened and the little boy froze. He turned and hugged Bess tightly. "Thank you," he said.

"You gotta stand up to bullies, OK?"

The little boy said nothing more.

"Kid, you comin'?" The bus driver seemed impatient. The little boy climbed up the steps, the door closed, and the bus pulled away.

Bess continued to walk to her bus. It was a warm August day and she wanted another shower when she got home.

Home. It was a funny word. This place didn't feel like home.

Bess put the old key into the decrepit deadbolt. The door around the lock was green, but had been several colors over the last decade. Was that blue? Red? Chips of paint flecked off as the door creaked open.

"Bess, is that you?"

"Yeah, Ma." Bess walked past the decayed foyer and unopened boxes. Six years, and they still weren't unpacked.

"Bess," her mother said, "how was your day?" Her words were slurred.

Bess walked into the tiny kitchen where her mother sat, wobbly in her chair. A cigarette dangled from her lips as she tried to balance a finger of vodka in a low ball glass. Bess ignored her and went to the refrigerator. "I see you didn't go shopping, Mom."

Her mother put her cigarette down and finished the vodka. "I got busy."

Bess scoured the cabinets and found some canned beans and corn. "Guess it'll have to do." Sounds of the latest pop band permeated the kitchen. Bess dug into her pocket and picked up her phone. "Hello?"

"Hey, Bessy! Whatcha up to?"

"Hey, Christine. Just fixing dinner."

"Cool. Hey, I was just wondering if you're coming to the party Friday."

Bess sighed. "You know I don't like those parties. Besides, I have to train."

"Paolo is going to be there." Christine's voice simply sang with every word.

Bess rolled her eyes. "Christine, I seriously doubt he wants a girl like me. I mean, he was dating Linda-Marie last June. Why would he want to date me? I'm not girly like that. Besides, sweaty gym shirts and sports bras do not attract boys."

"You're wrong, Bess. He totally digs you. He talks all the time about how you helped him pass English last year."

"I don't know."

"Look, you lose all the games you don't play, right?"

"Christine—"

Bess' mother began to cry.

"I—I'll think about, OK? I gotta go." Bess hung up and went to her mother. She knelt at her feet. "What's wrong, Ma?"

"You're so strong. Like your father… he would be… so proud of you right now."

Bess hugged her mother. "You hungry, Ma?"

She kept crying softly into Bess' shirt.

*   *   *

"Harder, Bess, harder." Michael was in quite the mood. "Christ, Bess, you hit like a girl!"

Bess tried to punch the bag harder while maintaining her speed. She released a furious round of uppercuts.

"Nice! That's the way to go. Time," Michael barked.

Bess took her mouthpiece out and took a deep breath. Michael handed her a water bottle. She was glistening with sweat.

"Good, Bess, good. You gotta hit 'em hard. A lot of girls don't train properly in the abdomen. You stick it to 'em there and they'll crumble like bacon."

Bess nodded in between gulping water.

"You sign up for the tournament yet?"

Bess shook her head.

Michael lifted his left eyebrow. "What? The deadline is Monday, Bess."

"I don't have the money just yet. Things are tight."

Michael pursed his lips. He looked as if he'd swallowed a lot of anger in his life. "Alright. Hit the showers."

Bess turned to walk away.

"Hey, Bess," Michael called to her. "Look, I know it's a lot, but you're getting so much better. If you can come up with the dough, I think you could go far, see?"

Bess could feel the heat in her cheeks. Everyone kept telling her there was no shame in poverty, so why were these moments so frequent? She nodded.

"Alright, kid." Michael tousled her hair and then left.

How was she going to come up with the money? It seemed hopeless.

Deep in thought, she proceeded to the women's locker room. Something wasn't right. She turned around to see a black man, thin and well groomed, staring at her. When their eyes met he smiled. It creeped her out, forcing her to the protection of the locker room.

When she returned, showered and dressed, Bess looked around for the man. Relieved not to have seen him, she headed for the door. She took two steps out of the locker room before she noticed him.

"Excuse me," he started, "is your name Elizabeth? Elizabeth Frasier?" He smiled warmly.

"Yes, I'm Elizabeth Frasier." She hoped polite interaction would help hide her fear. Every now and again, some guy would try to hit on her at the boxing gym. Most backed off when they found out she was 17. Most.

"My name is Ulysses Jones. I knew your father."

Her jaw dropped.

"Are you alright?"

"Y-yeah," she lied. "How did you know my father?"

"Your father—James and I were in graduate school together."

"How did you find me?"

"Your father loved boxing. He took me down here once, many years ago, when we were working on our dissertations. He told me it cleared his head to work out here."

Bess started to smile. It was a rare occurrence that she heard stories about her father.

"I was in town and, well, I missed him, so I thought I'd visit. Then I see this handsome young woman punching a bag, the spitting image of Dr. James Frasier." His smile boiled over into laughter. "I tell myself 'that's got to be Jimmy's little girl.'"

It was infectious, his laugh. Bess started laughing too, but then the smile disappeared.

"I'm sorry, am I keeping you?"

"No."

"I would love to buy you a soda or something. Would that be alright?"

Ulysses was charming and his smile was infectious. Tired and lonely, Bess gave into her curiosity and his charm. "Sure."

They walked three blocks to a coffee shop, which was old and run down like everything else. They took a seat and ordered two coffees. "I didn't know kids drank coffee. See what happens when you become an academic?" He smiled at her.

"Tell me about my father."

Ulysses eyes looked past her, as if he could see her father standing behind their booth. "Your father and I met our first year in graduate school, historiography. Good man. We studied together and became friends. Him from Boston, me from Detroit." Ulysses laughed. "Even then, after history, he loved boxing best of all."

Bess smiled at that.

"Until the day you were born. Everything became second to you."

Bess felt her cheeks warm at the compliment.

"My, did he love you." Ulysses' eyes sparkled as he spoke. "We were working on our dissertations when you were born. I think he bought 100 cigars, passed them out to everyone. I mean everyone!"

They both laughed at that.

"He even disrupted a seminar to give them out. He was so proud."

"What happened after that?" Bess asked.

"What always happens. He got a job on the east coast, I got a job in Texas. We drifted apart. I'm in town for a conference and I remembered the gym, so I came by." Ulysses sighed. "Don't really know why."

"Did you know my mother?"

Ulysses' smile disappeared. He looked down for a moment, composed himself, then smiled again. "I met her a couple of times."

"Oh."

Ulysses reached out and touched her arm. "Your father loved her very much, and she loved him."

Bess smiled blandly.

"How is your mother?"

She was shattered when Dad died. She abandoned me and crawled up into a bottle, waiting to die herself. That's what Bess wanted to say. "She's fine," is what she actually said.

Ulysses looked at his watch and his eyes grew big. "I've got to go, but this has been wonderful." He rose, pulled out his wallet and dropped a twenty dollar bill on the table. He then gave her a card. "Your father got me through grad school. I'm a historian because of him. Call me if you need anything, day or night. I can't promise I'll always be able to help, but I'll do what I can." He stuck out his hand to shake.

Bess got up and hugged him tightly.

*   *   *

Bess couldn't believe she was doing this. How did she ever let Christine talk her into this? This was going to be the worst night of her life.

Her phone rang.

"Hello? Ma?" Bess answered, "No, I'm not at school. Remember, Michael scheduled extra practice? I'm at the gym."

Bess strained to listen over the loud music.

"A-ha. A-ha. Alright, Ma. I'll be home a little late, OK? Love ya, bye."

Bess couldn't believe she had just lied to her mom. "OUCH!"

"Well hold still while I curl your hair, dummy."

Bess sat in a chair at Christine's house, listening to music and getting ready for the party. "I hate you, you know that?" Christine was putting the finishing touches on the ring of soft, blond curls in Bess' hair. "Your hair is so pretty and you fit into my little sister's jeans. Now I *really* hate you."

They both giggled.

Bess wore the tightest jeans they could find at Christine's house and a black satin top and jean jacket. Christine did Bess' make-up, too. They gossiped the whole afternoon, while getting ready and on the way to the party.

It was in a well-to-do part of town. Three stories, old growth trees, large back yard and a pool. Of course, the parents weren't there.

"I'll get us drinks," Christine announced.

"OK, nothing too strong."

Christine rolled her eyes.

Bess stood in the foyer, looking at about a hundred kids dancing, talking and making out. The music was loud and the lights were off, except for a couple of lamps.

Christine returned with two plastic cups. "What is it?"

"Just cola," Christine replied.

Bess took a drink. It was strong. Too strong. She didn't know what to do, so she swallowed it. "What the hell, Christine? I said nothing strong!"

"Is it too strong? I just put some rum in it." Christine's innocent face belied her character.

Bess sighed.

"Let's mingle," Christine announced.

The party was a mix of kids from several local high schools. The girls walked around the entire ground floor of the house and outside. They saw couples going upstairs but didn't themselves. Those rooms were for people who wanted privacy.

They were outside ogling the hot guys on the football team, who were talking to some pretty girls Bess felt were out of her league. "Oh my *Lord*. Bess, look." Christine tugged on Bess' right arm and pointed.

Paolo was talking to some guys neither Bess nor Christine knew. He was wearing his green and black lettermen jacket, which looked brand new. The other boys wore purple jackets, so were clearly from another school.

"Let's go talk to him," Christine squeaked.

"*No.*"

"Come on."

Bess was adamant. In no uncertain terms was she going over to him; that would *never* happen.

"*Oh my gosh*, he's coming over here," Christine whispered excitedly.

Paolo's lanky six foot frame sauntered over to Bess. His complexion was bronzed, like a Greek god. Many people wondered what race he was. Arab? Samoan? Latin? Of course Bess knew, because she had tutored him before. His father was Italian and his mother was black. It didn't matter to her though, she just kept thinking about falling asleep in those mighty arms.

"Hey Bess, I didn't think you went to parties."

She melted at his smile. "Christine said I should get out more."

Christine just stood there with a dumb smile on her face. "Hey Christine, would you freshen my drink?" Bess asked.

Snapped back to reality, she said, "Oh, yeah, freshen. Sure. I'll be back."

Bess and Paolo were now alone, and she had to actively suppress the urge to kiss him.

"Did you want to go somewhere and talk? It's nice at the other end of the pool," Paolo said.

"Oh, OK." Bess smiled.

"How's the training going?" he asked as they walked.

"It's fine."

"I heard there's a big tournament coming up. Are you going to enter?"

How do you impress a guy by telling him you're broke? "I'm thinking about it."

Paolo became excited. "No, Bess. You've gotta. It would be awesome."

"Well…"

"Did you enter last year?"

"Yeah. Lost my first match, then the consolation fight. Wasn't really impressive." Bess grinned sheepishly.

"I'm sure you'll do better this time. Besides, you look ripped. Let me see your bicep?" He moved around her to remove her jacket. He was gentle and slow. His cologne smelled wonderful, as did his clean hair. "Now, let me see those guns," Paolo said playfully.

Bess' blouse buttoned at the wrist, which she unbuttoned, then rolled up.

"Man, you are cut."

Bess always thought boys liked soft girls with curves. Was she wrong? He touched her elbow, sliding his fingers up her arm. A streak of electricity flashed through her body. Her heart pounded.

"Bess, you would hurt any other girl in that ring. You gotta fight. You just gotta." His eyes were bright and full.

"There you two are," Christine said. "I was looking for you."

"Tell this girl to enter that boxing tournament."

"Oh, I don't know," Christine said. "Not really interested in the whole sweating and punching and bruising thing." She had a twisted look on her face. "But Bess is awesome. Are you gonna enter?"

Bess felt awkward being the center of attention. "I don't know." She was too embarrassed to admit she didn't have the money.

Paolo jokingly groaned. "Listen, you would kick butt." He helped Bess put her jacket back on. "You'd walk away with that trophy, I'm sure of it."

She locked eyes with him. What Bess saw there was more than excitement, more than faith in her fists. She saw respect and affection. "You really think so?"

"I do."

She felt her cheeks flush again, so started playing with her blond curls. They talked some more while Christine hovered between three clicks of kids. Paolo came back and forth, talking with his friends too, but when he came back to her she had his undivided attention. He listened to her, laughed at her jokes, even brushed her hand once. For the first time in a very long while, Bess felt pretty and wanted. Only her father had made her feel like that before.

The party ended like all parties end. Bess and Paolo hugged goodnight, and he kissed her cheek. The warmth of his body felt good against hers. When they parted, she wondered why he had to be such a gentleman.

The next day it was back to training. She worked on footwork, punch combos and lifted weights. She had been coming here since she was 13 years old and full of rage because of the death of her father. At first the bag was a way to work out her grief, then a way to honor his love of the sport. Finally, she grew to love it herself, in its own right.

She took a break and spotted another woman in the gym. "Michael, who's that?"

"I think she's new, up from New York. Tonya, I think." Michael took out a pair of gloves. "Break time over, Bess. Let's get to work."

Bess worked the rest of the afternoon in the ring. When she finished, she hit the showers. She was putting her shoes on when the new girl came in. Tonya stalked across the room like a cat. She peered down every row. She wore black sneakers, blue jeans and a t-shirt that said BAD TO THE BONE. Two other girls accompanied her.

"You're new here," Bess began. "My name is Bess. It'll be nice to have more girls around." She put her hand out for Tonya to shake.

Tonya looked Bess up and down. "This your gym?"

"Yeah, I train with Michael."

Tonya slowly shook her head. "This isn't *your* gym anymore. From now on, this is *my* gym. You're just a squirrel, tryin' to get a nut. Understand?"

Tonya's breath was hot and foul. What was going on? Bess' heart beat wildly. She didn't feel safe, anymore. "Look, I don't know what I did to offend you, but—"

"No buts, chick. For the three weeks I'm down here, this will be *my* home. Understand?"

Tonya stepped forward and Bess stepped back. When she left, Bess tried to figure out what she had done to upset Tonya. She played it through over and over in her head.

When she got home her mom was cooking dinner. Ground beef was browning on the stove, smelling of onions and garlic.

Her mom sipped from a tumbler of ice and vodka as she stirred. "How was the gym?"

"Oh, it was good," she lied.

"Dinner'll be done in 15 minutes."

During dinner, Mom switched to wine. The spaghetti was very good. Pleasant dinners like these were rare, so Bess got up the nerve to ask. "So, Mom," Bess began, "there's this big boxing tournament for girls in a couple of weeks. I want to enter."

"You know how I feel about you boxing. I only allow it because your father loved it so."

Bess took a deep breath. "I know, Ma, but it would mean so much to me."

Mom took a long draw from her tumbler of wine. "I don't want you getting hurt, Elizabeth."

"Ma, everyone wears head gear, the fights are only three rounds."

Bess' mother sighed. "Alright, Elizabeth, you can fight. Just be careful of your face. A woman's place in the world is made by her face."

Bess jumped from her seat, bounded over to her mother and kissed her cheek. "Thank you, Mom. Thank you, thank you, thank you."

"Sure. How much are the entrance fees?"

"$250."

The smile evaporated from her mother's face. "Sweetie, I paid the bills with the disability check. I have nothing."

Bess felt a vacuous pit form in her abdomen. "What?"

Her mother had a pained expression. "Sweetie, we're broke."

*   *   *

Bess didn't go to the gym for three days. What was the point? She couldn't enter the tournament, so why train? She just went to school, which was something perfunctory for Bess; a burden at best.

"Hey Bess, what's cooking?" It was Paolo. Wonderful Paolo.

"Oh nothing."

"Hey, can I pick your brain about that AP history exam tomorrow?"

"Sure. Let's walk and talk."

It was the end of the school day. Many students had gone, so the halls were almost empty. Paolo had a confused look on his face. "So, the test is on Queen Elizabeth I of England."

"Yeah."

"I don't get something. She ignores the Spanish and the French for, like, twenty years. She barely consents to allow volunteers to go to the Netherlands. She's totally anti-war."

"That's right. She avoided fighting at all costs."

"But then the O'Neil rebellion started in Ireland, in… um…"

She laughed. "1597."

"Right, 1597, and all of a sudden she's all in. What gives?"

"Elizabeth avoided war for thirty years. Even when the Spanish Armada came, she decided not to escalate things, allowing pirates to disrupt shipping and maybe steal some Mexican silver. But she didn't want war."

"So why go all 'first person shooter' in Ireland?"

"She had pardoned O'Neil before. She had tried three or four different kinds of governing techniques. Nothing would placate the Irish. When she heard he was rebelling again, after everything she'd done, Elizabeth had had enough."

Paolo looked confused. Suddenly, his eyes got big and his mouth dropped. "Oh, she just got tired of everyone's crap."

41

Bess laughed. "Yeah, you could say that. After 1597, there was no amount she wouldn't spend, no action she wouldn't take to keep Ireland."

"Wow, Bess, you really know your stuff."

"Thanks. My dad taught Tudor History at the local community college. He named me after Queen Elizabeth."

"Wow."

"He admired her because there was nothing she wouldn't do to get what she wanted."

"This was helpful, Bess. Thanks a lot, but I'm late to swim practice." He kissed her forehead.

There was nothing she wouldn't do to get what she wanted.

Bess walked outside the school and sat on one of the front steps. She rummaged through her backpack. Her eyes lit up when she found the crumpled card. She took her cellphone out and dialed. "Hello, Professor Jones? It's Bess."

*   *   *

"Ladies and gentlemen, welcome to the 3rd annual all-city amateur women's boxing tournament. This is the quarter-finals." The announcer made the fight seem as impressive as he could. The city arena, an old building from the 1930s, didn't seat more than 4,000 people. They were lucky if 300 were in here tonight.

"You ready for this?" Michael asked.

Bess nodded.

DING DING.

Bess circled her opponent. She was a soft fighter, with rolled shoulders. The girl jabbed slowly. Bess replied with some jabs of her own. She circled her, looking for weakness.

Her opponent let loose a combo of punches that staggered Bess out of surprise. She wrapped her arms around her chest and face for protection. She took blow after blow. Bess grabbed the other girl's arm and locked it, forcing the referee to break them up.

When he let them go at it again, Bess stepped up, jabbed twice with her left, then landed a solid cross. The girl staggered. Her eyes looked dazed. Bess pounced on her, landing blows to her midsection and head.

The bell rang. Both fighters went back to their coaches.

"You rang her bell, Bess, do it again."

Bess nodded.

DING DING.

Bess almost ran out of her corner. She hit the other girl with combinations of crosses, hooks and jabs. She was unrelenting. Bess was full of energy.

DING DING.

Bess danced around the other girl, laying jabs and crosses intermittently. By the end, the other girl was sucking wind, tired of chasing Bess around the ring.

"With a score of 30-27, 30-27, 28-27, the winner is... Elizabeth Frasier!"

*   *   *

"You should have been there," Bess said. "It was amazing. I danced around that ring like a butterfly. She couldn't touch me."

Paolo smiled broadly. They held hands as they walked in the park. "I'm sorry I missed it. I had a swim meet."

Bess looked up at Paolo, hope in her eyes. "You'll come to the semi-final, won't you? Tonight?"

"Of course." He drew near her, putting his hands around her waist. "I wouldn't want my girlfriend to beat me up." He then kissed her, long and hard on the mouth. His tongue was delicious against hers. She could feel his heartbeat... among other things.

"I do like doing that," he said, and played with her golden curls.

"I like it, too. Come here and kiss me again."

Everything was perfect. He got an A on that test, thanks to Bess. He was so happy he kissed her. She kissed back. So much had happened in a week.

"I've got to get home," she said.

They said their goodbyes and Bess went home to pick up her gear. She arrived to her mother watching television and drinking vodka.

"Hi, Mom." Bess moved past her as quickly as possible, grabbed her bag and headed for the door.

"Where you going?" her mother slurred.

"I gotta fight."

"How? We don't have no money for fights."

"Um, I got a scholarship." It was kind of true. Bess kissed her mother on the forehead. "I've gotta go, Mom, love ya."

*   *   *

"Ladies and gentlemen, welcome to the semi-finals. In this corner, weighing in at 132 pounds, is Bess Frasier."

The crowd clapped politely. Bess looked around as the announcer spoke, and she spotted Tonya. "Hey Michael, how'd she do in the first round?"

Michael looked at Tonya, then at Bess. "Knockout, third round."

"In an amateur fight? I ain't never heard such a thing."

"Worry about Tonya in the finals."

DING DING.

The fighter this time was tall, thick. She walked right up to Bess and swung. Fortunately, Bess ducked. The taller woman chased Bess throughout rounds 1 and 2. Bess ducked, jabbed and racked up points. She technically outperformed the taller boxer. When the bell rang, Bess felt good.

"Alright, you're 180 seconds away from the finals. Just keep away from her, OK?" Michael was deadly serious.

"Yeah, of course." Bess was a little distracted, as she didn't see Paolo.

DING DING.

Bess danced around, jabbed and swung an occasional uppercut into the woman's ribs, but she was distracted. Where was Paolo? He said he would come. Why wasn't he here? Then she saw Tonya get up and leave the fight with her two friends. Where was she going?

THUD.

Bess had the wind knocked out of her. Her opponent connected with a solid punch to the ribs. She couldn't breathe.

"Bess, get out of there," Michael cried.

Confused and disoriented, Bess started to back up. The bigger boxer kept coming after her. She landed lefts and rights, jabs and crosses. Every blow hurt worse than the last. Finally, the bell rang and Bess limped back to her coach.

"What the heck happened?" Michael barked.

"I got distracted," Bess said as she took her gloves off.

"She could have killed you." He poked her forehead with his index finger. "Use your head."

"Ladies and gentlemen, with scores of 30-27, 29-28, and 28-29, the winner is... Bess Frasier!"

She won. She was in the finals, but Bess didn't celebrate. Where was Paolo? She hugged her opponent, said thank you to the crowd and went back to the locker room. Her side ached where she'd received the first punch. In the shower, eyes closed, Bess let the hot water run over her. Suddenly, she heard clapping.

"Well, well, well. Looks like Goldilocks is a real fighter."

Bess shut the water off and turned around. "What do you want, Tonya?"

"I told you to stay out of my way, didn't I?" Tonya walked into the shower stalls, her friends at her flanks. "Now, Goldilocks, you'll have to learn."

Bess put her towel on and tried to move past them, but they blocked her way. Bess was tired of feeling bad, of worrying about other people thought. She was tired of Tonya. "Anything you have to say to me can wait until we're in the ring."

Tonya's friend sucker-punched her.

"You're gonna learn, Blondie."

*   *   *

Bess laid on the floor of the shower for half an hour before someone came looking for her. "Bess? BESS? Are you descent?"

"Michael... help... me."

His footsteps got closer. She wished she could have covered herself, but she was too weak.

"Oh Christ and all his angels."

The look on his face told Bess everything. It was a look of pain, pity, and horror that reflected the harsh locker room lights as she laid nude and battered, with her golden hair cut off and strewn wildly all over the floor.

She looked up to see Michael grab her towel and cover her. Gently, he picked her up and carried her to her stuff. "Are you alright, honey?"

"No, but I will be."

He sat her down next to her locker. Her things were strewn all over the floor. "I'm gonna call the police."

"No." A flush of anger rose in Bess. "Don't. I'm fine. I slipped, that's all."

Michael raised an eyebrow. "You… slipped?"

Bess sighed. "Yes. I slipped."

"Did you accidentally cut your hair off, too?"

Bess glared at Michael. "I can handle it, Michael. Just get out of here, OK?"

Michael huffed, then began picking up her clothes. When he was done he walked out.

"Hey Michael," Bess called, "thanks for not being creepy."

"Is that what you're worried about? Sheesh. I'll be outside when you're ready."

Bess got dressed, gathered her things and walked out. She was intimidated before, even a little scared. She was hurt that Paolo didn't come. More than anything else, she was tired.

Michael drove her back home. "You gonna be alright?"

"Yeah, I think so."

Michael looked Bess up and down. There was affection and love in his eyes. "Put some ice on that eye, OK?"

She smiled. "Thanks."

Bess dropped her things in the kitchen and got a glass of water. In the living room, her mom was passed out on the couch.

"Hey, Mom."

She didn't move.

"Mom?" Bess shook her. "Mom?" Her skin was cold and clammy. She reeked of vodka.

"MOM."

*   *   *

The room was uncomfortable and sterile, but hospital waiting rooms were never comfortable.

"Bess?" Christine walked in with her parents. "Oh my God, Bess, I'm so sorry." They hugged. "My phone was off all day Sunday. I didn't see your texts until second period. I came as fast as I could."

"Are you alright?" Christine's mother asked. "We brought some food." She passed Bess homemade sandwiches in wax paper.

"Thank you, ma'am." Bess took a bite. She hadn't realized how hungry she was.

"We want you to stay with us until your mother's out of the hospital," Christine's mother said.

Bess felt a flush of heat rise in her face, tears welling. "Thank you, ma'am. I'd like that."

"Has she woken up?" Christine asked.

"They woke her up when she got here. Then they pumped the alcohol out of her stomach. She was up briefly after that so they could watch her, keep her stable. She fell asleep a couple of hours ago." Bess fought back tears.

"Oh My God, Bess. What happened to your hair?" Christine asked, obviously horrified.

"I can't talk about it right now. I'm fine." She smiled blandly.

"I got you some more coffee." Michael turned the corner with two large cups from a local chain.

"This is Mike, my trainer," Bess said to Christine and her family. "He's been with me since I found her." Introductions were made all around. They talked about Bess' mother. How she had suffered alcohol poisoning. How they had got to her just in time. How they were doing other tests, just to make sure she hadn't suffered a stroke or heart attack while unconscious.

After a while Christine and her parents left. Bess promised Christine she would keep her phone on, day and night.

Exhausted, Bess sat next to Mike. "I'm tired, coach. So tired."

Mike placed his hand behind her head and stroked her remaining hair. "I know you are. You've been here two days."

"I'm not talking about that. I'm talking about taking care of my mom. I'm talking about feeling like I don't fit in. I'm talking about boys, and missing my dad, and all that crap." Tears began to fall. "I just want to rest. I want to be normal. I want to be a cheerleader or something, I don't know."

Michael took a hard swallow of coffee. "You've had it bad, kid. It wasn't fair that your dad died when you were ten. It wasn't fair that you got saddled with a mom you had to take care of. Things would have been a lot easier had you fallen in love with tennis, or ballet, or cheerleading." He chuckled at that one. "But you didn't, and you keep plugging along. You're a survivor Bess, like that Queen Elizabeth your dad named you after."

Bess smiled a little.

"Look, I've been a boxer all my life. I don't know nothin' but the ring. I do know this, though: at the end of the day, you've got two clear choices. When things go wrong you can either throw the towel in or answer the bell."

Bess looked at Michael, awed. She saw no guile or subtlety in his face, just the truth as he understood it. It was hard and uncomfortable, but it was a constant, and that was somehow comforting.

"Elizabeth Frasier?" a nurse called.

Bess stood.

"Your mother is awake now. You can see her."

Bess followed the nurse back to her mother's room. There, her mother sat up in bed, her chin covered in dried black matter. Bess ran to hug her.

"I'm alright, child, I'm alright," her mother said.

"I'm sorry, Mom. I'm sorry. I'll never leave you again. I should have been there. I—"

"Shhh," her mother said. "It's alright. You know, I should be the one apologizing to you."

Bess pulled away. "What?"

"Sit down. We have to talk."

Bess found a chair.

"Bess, I should apologize to you. I haven't been a mother to you for at least six of these years your father has been gone. I gave up on life. I gave up on you.

"Your father broke my heart when he died. I was more angry with him than I was hurt he had gone. I spent the first two years after his death resenting him. I spent the next five feeling sorry for myself and resenting you."

"Me? Why resent me?"

"Because you looked like him more every day. You have his eyes and nose. He loved you so much."

"Ma, I don't know what to do." The tears began again. "I have this fight and I'm so tired. I just want to go home and sleep. I want to be normal."

"Elizabeth Paula-Ann Frasier," her mother said sternly, "you are not normal. You are special. I know it. You know it. Your trainer knows it. If your father heard you talking like this he would be ashamed."

Bess' eyes widened and her mouth dried up.

"You are a fighter, so go fight. It's what you do best." Her mother closed her eyes. "I'm going to take a nap now."

Bess didn't know what to do.

"Don't worry about me, you've got training to do."

Eventually, Bess' mother began to snore. Bess sat there, taking it all in. The only thing that ever made sense after her father's death was that ring. She got up and kissed her mother on the forehead. "Love ya, Ma."

She went back to the waiting room. Michael looked up at her. "How's she doing?"

"She's fine. We've got training to do."

"What?"

*   *   *

The next three days were grueling. Bess ran, lifted weights, trained on the bag. She also went to school and visited her mom, who got better every day. Word had gotten out about what had happened to Bess' mom and the whole school rallied around her. She saw Paolo in history class, but he was sheepish and didn't make eye contact.

That Thursday Bess trained lightly in preparation for the fight. Mike was giving her instructions while she did some sit-ups. "Tonya is lightning fast. She can punch, too. Keep your guard up, wait to counter-punch."

Out of the corner of her eye she saw Paolo. In her gym. His smile lit up the room. "What's up, champ?"

Michael moved in front. "Excuse me, this ain't no social call. We're training for a fight. You'll have to leave."

"It's OK Michael, he can stay," Bess said. "Go fill up my water bottle, please?"

Michael got the hint. Bess kept doing sit-ups.

"Hey, I heard about your mom. I—I just wanted to say how sorry I was, am. How sorry I am." He was clearly very uncomfortable.

"Why weren't you at the fight Saturday night?"

Paolo shifted, grinning like a boy in trouble. "I don't know. It got pretty intense between us and I just felt—"

"Felt what?" Bess continued her sit ups.

"I don't know, constricted. On lockdown. I needed space."

The silence that followed evidently unnerved Paolo, so he broke it. "Say something."

"What's there to say?"

"What?"

"Look, Paolo, I like you, but I've got bigger things to deal with than your ego. If you can't handle me the way I am, if I can't depend on you, maybe we should just be study buddies."

Paolo looked like he had no idea what to say, so he turned and walked away.

She wanted to cry, but wouldn't give him the satisfaction. She got up, went to the lockers with every intention of taking a shower. She passed by a mirror and looked at her hair in uneven clumps. She went to her locker and got a pair of electric clippers. Back at the mirror she shaved her head. What was left was a short crop of blond peach fuzz. Then she took a shower.

*　　　　*　　　　*

"Ladies and gentlemen, welcome to the 3rd annual all-city women's boxing championship. In the near corner, at 147 pounds, we have contender No. 1, Tonya Shore." Applause sprinkled the auditorium.

"In the far corner, at 143 pounds, we have contender No. 2, Elizabeth Frasier." Thunderous applause echoed from the rafters.

"What's that about?" Bess asked.

Michael smiled. "Your friend Christine apparently told the entire school. Congrats kid, you've got a home court advantage."

Bess just stared right at Tonya, who stared right back at her. When the referee finished giving instructions, Bess went back to her corner one last time.

"Counter-punch, don't get flat footed, OK?"

DING DING.

Bess came out dancing around the ring. Tonya stalked her like prey. A few jabs were thrown. Bess got in a hook to the ribs. The crowd cheered wildly. They continued to dance for about half the round.

Tonya jabbed repeatedly, then followed those up with a cross that startled Bess. She staggered back and Tonya was right on her. Crosses and hooks flew at Bess' face. She tried to counter, but the blows were too fast. She grabbed Tonya's waist, tangling the two.

"Nice haircut, Goldilocks."

The referee separated them, then let them at it again. Tonya pounced with a flurry of blows to Bess' face.

DING DING.

Bess' head throbbed. She drank some water. "You've gotta move, girl. Move," Michael instructed.

Bess nodded. The bell called her back to the ring.

She danced around again, sending light jabs into Tonya's face. Tonya didn't even try to dodge or block. Bess jabbed again. Suddenly, an uppercut caught her in the stomach. She lost her balance. Tonya jumped in and started pounding her again, body and face.

Bess tried to block the punches, cover her face, but it wasn't working. Tonya was too fast. Bess could hear the crowd gasping. She tried to step back but took a cross in the face as she did. Her legs turned to water and she hit the ground.

"1..."

"Get up, Bess!"

"2..."

"Stay down, Goldilocks."

"3... 4..."

"I'm so tired. I just want to rest..."

"5..."

"You're a fighter. Go fight. It's what you do best."

"6..."

"You either throw in the towel or you answer the bell."

"7… 8…"

Finally, Bess was standing.

"Go to your corner."

Michael checked her eyes. "Are you alright?"

"Yeah. Your strategy ain't working Michael. I'm tryin' something new."

Michael looked at Bess oddly. "Yeah, try it. Just don't get killed."

Bess went back to the center of the ring. The two touched gloves, restarting the fight. Bess swung wildly, forcing Tonya to backpedal. She threw haymakers and uppercuts. She stopped caring about defense. She went after Tonya's face.

Crosses, hooks, and uppercuts went everywhere. Tonya protected her face and then punched back. The crowd went wild as they stopped dancing and stood there, beating each other.

Tonya landed some blows, but so did Bess.

DING DING.

"What in the name of Christ are you doing?"

Bess drank some water. "She's too fast for counter-punching. If I have a chance, it's got to be a street brawl. Blow for blow."

"She'll win that way, too."

Bess looked at Michael. "Yeah, but I'll get my shots in, too. Who knows, one might land just right."

DING DING.

"You've lost your mind, Bess."

Bess shrugged as she walked to the center of the ring. She motioned with her left hand, *come on.*

The two threw blows like gladiators. Attendants gasped and screamed. There was no pretense of art or technical skill. They were trying to hurt each other. Bess took several crosses to her head. Her vision blurred, but she landed cross after cross into Tonya's face.

The crowd's voices thundered, but Bess didn't care. In Tonya's head gear was the face of everything gone wrong in her life. Sometimes Bess punched her mom, other times it was Mike. Sometimes it was a teacher or student she hated. A couple of times it was Paolo.

Bess began mixing her punches with uppercuts to the body. Her combos were landing. Tonya looked wobbly. Bess sent blow after blow. Tonya swung wild and Bess sent her to the canvass with an uppercut.

The crowd cheered so loud that Bess couldn't hear her thoughts.

As the referee began the count, Tonya started to crawl. By three she was on all fours. By five she was on one knee. By seven she was standing.

The referee sent her to her coach, who looked at her and sent her back.

To the end, Bess thought, *to the end*.

The two touched gloves. In the middle of the ring the two pounded each other. Every legal punch imaginable was thrown. Every punch received.

DING DING.

The two boxers collapsed into each other's arms.

"You've got balls, Goldilocks, I'll give you that."

"What the heck is keeping you up, Tonya?"

"I have no idea."

The women separated and went back to their corners.

Michael took Bess' head gear off. "I'm proud of you."

"I'm proud of myself."

Bess waited for the announcer to declare the winner. It took longer than usual as the referee conferred with each judge, then sent the card to the announcer.

"Ladies and gentlemen, please forgive the delay. We have determined the winner of the 3rd annual all-city women's boxing tournament."

Audience members, as well as the people in the ring, began to grumble and gossip.

"With the judges scoring it 29-27, 28-27, and 28-28, for the first time in tournament history we have a draw and co-champions!"

The grumblings turned to guffaws and a smattering of boos. Michael threw Bess' headgear down. "You got robbed."

Bess smiled, a large powder blue ring around her left eye slowly turning purple. "No I didn't." She walked over to Tonya and offered her hand. "Good fight."

Tonya studied Bess for a moment, then hugged her. "I owe you because of the hair."

"Yeah, you do."

They raised each other's hand in victory.

DRAWING HEARTS
Melissa Koons

Critical eyes assess
physical imperfections,
ashamed of these flaws
that should be hidden.
Compared to an unattainable ideal,
I draw hearts
on curves I should hate,
and love my skin and bones.
I smile at beautiful
wide hips, thick thighs
that dance to an ideal
rhythm of their own.

I smile at beautiful
physical imperfections
and love my skin and bones.
Ashamed of their flaws,
critical eyes
should be hidden.
When compared to an unattainable
ideal, wide hips, thick thighs
are curves I should hate.
But I draw hearts
and dance to an ideal
that is my own.

Love your skin and bones.
Don't compare to an unattainable
ideal that should be hidden
and ashamed of its flaws.
Dance to an ideal
rhythm that is your own
with wide hips, thick thighs.
Critical eyes assess
and draw hearts
on curves you shouldn't hate.
Smile at beautiful
physical imperfections.

A PLACE TO BELONG
Charlie Godwyne

Moving to a more liberal city really helped. I was raised in a conservative area that was very gendered, and my body always felt out of place. Once I moved to a more relaxed place and joined a support group, I learned that any body is welcome with any identity, and this is something to be celebrated. I began a process that was long and arduous, of acknowledging my own dissonance with my body and experimenting with what made me feel comfortable and how I wanted to express myself day-to-day. The worst part was that for years I didn't have a single day of feeling like I fit in with my own group, with myself. Membership One. How would I ever survive in a world that judged me at every turn if I couldn't accept myself? That stage felt like it would last forever.

It took time, blessed time, to convince my psyche that I was safe, accepted, neutral in my surroundings. If I walked around like I knew what I was doing and nothing about my appearance should be of any concern to anyone, then people generally acted like it was none of their concern. Anonymity in public was normalcy, not drawing stares or comments. Some days when I fought a long battle with the mirror before leaving the apartment, I'd go outside to see that no one was reacting to me, and by that reassurance I would be able to settle in, calm down and go about my day. That functionality got me through the day without the dissonance dogging me at every social interaction.

I came to the conclusion that having a name that was not clearly masculine or feminine would help my heart to rise to the surface of the tide instead of wincing at every crash of the waves. No more Joes and Janes. Now rise the Morgans, Taylors, Charlies and Jamies. The name conversion took a long time, and the legal transfer even longer, but having a name that gave me permission to fluctuate didn't pressure me to judge my body parts. I began to realize that I could still be a Charlie and not have to have a chest like this or that, hips of any certain size, hair like this, feet like that. I could sit at a coffee shop, and for all the world I would just be a Charlie drinking a cup of coffee. A simple act for other people, but for me this was a fundamentally transformative thing. No matter what I was at any point in time, I could still be a Charlie in that moment too. I could still be me, whatever that was.

So, after a solid five years of diligently insisting that I had to be gentle with myself no matter what I was feeling, I finally decided to do something to help the world, now that I had found my own acceptance. I had been writing fiction with characters of all bodies and identities, because as a child I found no stories with people like me as the hero. Even more than writing, I wanted to get out and do something, to be present in the world as the person I am. Just a human. It didn't take long to find a cause—the environment—and I only had to wait a week for a solidarity rally in my city.

I walked in the back, chanting that water is life, and when we stopped for the Native Americans leading the rally to sing a prayer for the planet, the rest of us raised our hands in silent support. I looked up at my hands against the blue sky. Just hands, no labels visible from this angle. I realized I would always be changing, and I smiled at those hands.

TO LET COOL
Jordan Felker

She crouched in the corner of the sofa
hidden in a swirl of blankets, a gate of pillows.
If she could have drawn her knees farther into herself,
she would have consumed them, absorbed and fused them
into her abdomen to mask it from the world.
What is it a stomach holds that is so precious and so
private?
Something to shield from the blows and batterings she
thought it might suffer
if she let fall her arms and opened herself to the
uncertainty.
She stewed there a while, thoughts simmering in the slow
but never exploding anxieties,
each thought bubbling   to the top
for its moment to disrupt the calm surface,
to make itself known with a roiling,   explosive
pressure and a satisfying, bubbly   pop.
She had been here before,
recognized the uncomfortable rising,
tried to cool panic with distraction—but denying bubbles
never actually
negates
their existence.
So the first of them began to burst
in sauce-spattering explosions—the bubbles growing

'til they overtook the very shape and size of her mind,
until she rose
from the nest of cushions that warmed her stew,
and padded, barefoot on the cool hardwood, to the
bathroom.

In the mirror, a woman of serene gaze, aquiline nose, and
bright
red lips to match the blush high on her cheeks.
The sight startled her into consciousness
of her feet on the floor—
hand on the doorframe.
She had forgotten that she looked like that.
Or perhaps she never knew.
And this version looked so calm, so poised, so—
Lines marked the crease that would pull back when she
smiled, and the folds
of her forehead if she lifted an eyebrow with skepticism
or disdain, or—heaven forbid—
amusement.
This woman, not girl, cool and wise,
not boiling in the corner of the sofa, blanched with her
anxieties.
To reconcile the two. To let cool
the boiling, to simmer into this graceful reflection.

HOW I LEARNED TO DANCE
Stacey Lorin Merkl

"It don't mean a thing, if it ain't got that swing…"

At 13 years old, I discovered swing in all its forms; the music, the dance, the culture. I was hooked. I fell in love and I fell hard. The music spoke deeply to my soul, to a part of my very being that had lived and breathed the music on a much deeper level than I was capable of understanding.

While my classmates listened to pop tunes on the radio, I began to study the sweet jive of Count Basie, Duke Ellington and Artie Shaw. Visions of Lindy Hop danced in my head as I watched videos of dancers, longing to be able to express myself and move with the freedom and joy I saw on screen.

At 15, I began taking lessons, and when I was old enough to drive and could get permission, Sunday nights I went out on the town. Putting on my best skirt and twisting my hair back, I would drive to an old club in town where, for one evening a week, we would be transported in time. The band was hot and the dancing was fast, and I was ready for the ride.

My soul moved with the music. I knew just what to do, but with all my vigor and passion there was one thing I lacked: confidence. I watched the others, I tapped my toes and snapped my fingers, but I spent much of the evening sitting, watching, wishing I could be dancing. I wished I could be more confident, more comfortable in my own skin, just… more. I kept telling myself that if I could look right, if I could be thinner, then I would feel more confident. I would wait until then. I would wait until I was someone different, someone… better.

These feelings of insecurity were part of a much longer history of not believing in myself or my abilities. From a very young age I can remember feeling ashamed of my body. Even as a small child I can remember feeling less than my classmates, feeling unworthy. Over the years these small insecurities would grow and mount into severe body image issues, and as I entered college they would lead to the development of an eating disorder.

I lived for much of my young adult life in a constant state of feeling not only not good enough, but also undeserving of joy. For many years as I struggled, I would actively avoid the things in life that brought me joy. Feeling unworthy, I told myself that as soon as I could change, I would join the others on the dance floor. As soon as I looked more like a "dancer," as soon as I was deserving—that was when I would dance.

After years of healing and work, I can honestly say that for the first time in my entire life, I truly love my body. I have learned throughout my healing and recovery process that many people feel the way that I felt: undeserving of joy, holding themselves back and feeling not good enough. Over the years I have fought hard to love myself, and it has now become my mission in life to help others learn to love themselves as well.

As the Founder & Executive Director of an organization whose sole mission is to promote positive body image to youth through theatre arts, one of the main lessons that we try to teach children is to embrace who they are. In order to fully teach young people this lesson, I had to question where in my own life I was holding back.

So, I began to dance. I challenged myself to start taking lessons again, to start going to as many dances and events as possible. I challenged myself to get on the dance floor, just as I was—right there and then, in that moment. At times it was difficult. Many nights I looked around and didn't see even one other dancer that looked like me. After all, society has all too often conditioned us that the words 'plus-sized' and 'dancer' do not belong in the same sentence. However, I continued to push myself and I continued to dance, and I have begun to feel proud to take on the stereotype of what a 'dancer' looks like. I have danced to the best swing bands in the world, Lindy Hopped in the hottest venues in NYC, and I have danced on the stage of the hallowed Apollo Theatre. I dance truly and I dance joyfully, and it all started with self-love.

Now that I have allowed myself to fully love and embrace my body, and live fully inside of it, I am one of the first people on the dance floor and often one of the last to leave. My soul cannot get enough, and by embracing myself I know that I am allowing one of the most sincere and honest forms of self-care: *joy*.

It's important that we not wait to live our lives until we reach some arbitrary goal or size or weight or standard; that we don't fall into the line of thinking that everything will magically be better once we 'fix' ourselves. It's important that we don't deprive ourselves of enjoying our lives because we don't think we deserve it. Be it wearing your bathing suit in public to cool off on a hot summer day, taking up a new activity you've always wanted to try, or getting on that dance floor and cutting loose, it's important to do what makes you happy. You deserve it.

What are the things in your own life that you want to do, that you're passionate about, that make you happy, and which you're putting off to another day? What are the things that you haven't been doing because you've convinced yourself you can't or you aren't worthy? Now is the time. I'm here to tell you that *you are worthy*. You deserve to do the things you want to do. You deserve to feel passionate. You deserve to be happy. You deserve to *dance*.

REFLECTIONS
Thomas A. Fowler

Stephanie Tao expected something unusual from an intergalactic portal. But a pane of reflective glass floating in space seemed odd, even for an event such as this. She stared, eager to open the pressure door and make her way toward the portal's entrance. Her gloves wrapped around the window framing, fingers clutching the metal circle surrounding the glass viewfinder. Her tight grip pressed against the thick padding of her exosuit.

Zero gravity pulled her legs back and up, floating toward the ceiling. As the thick soles of the massive boots hit the roof of the shuttle, she kicked her body back down. A familiar tinge in her knee surged through the ligaments. The searing pain had become all too familiar. This was her last time up in space, she knew it. Time had finally gotten the better of her. Her knee was the body saying it had seen enough.

Stephanie's last excursion was one for the record books. She was part of the first crew headed for direct contact with an unknown origin in space. Three years prior, Earth received a transmission; an invitation to a portal. It marked first contact between humans and an alien species. Stephanie remembered the worn chair she sat in the day they announced it to the crew. It was the day she found she'd be part of the crew headed for the transmission point.

Aboard the shuttle, her captain, Mike Crawford, floated next to her. "What does it do?"

Stephanie drifted toward the ceiling again. Mike placed his hand on her back to stabilize her. His hand remained for a moment.

"I'm fine, thank you," Stephanie said.

"Of course." He retreated, placing his hand to his side. He smiled at her. He'd put the exosuit helmet on already. The large viewfinder in the front profiled his jaw line. She'd appreciated his skills as a pilot, but had little respect for him being on this mission. He hadn't been tested. He was the company's poster boy; the joyful action figure, blonde-haired hero everyone could watch on the news. He was the heroic face of a space ranger to represent America.

"Knee feeling any better?" he asked.

"Fine for zero gravity," Stephanie replied.

She bent her knee, pulling the back of her heel against her thigh. She flexed it up and down to keep the blood flowing, forbidding the joint from locking up.

"If you're in too much pain, you don't have to go," Mike offered.

"Yes, I do," Stephanie said. "I'm the communications expert. I interpreted the message. Unless you understand the levels of syntax in the alien communication and how to speak without gender forms, everything will sound like gibberish to you. I assume you know how to speak without verb tension, right?"

"What?" Mike asked.

"It's why I was able to decipher the communication," Stephanie said.

"I was merely offering," he said.

"Do that for something small—a fuel check or air filter change—but not before one of the single most important moments in human history," Stephanie said.

She turned the handle on the pressure door.

"Did we get clearance?" Mike asked.

"Base, this is *The Sterna*, requesting permission for spacewalk to portal." She placed her exosuit helmet on.

"*Sterna,* this is Base. You are clear."

Stephanie pushed the right handle. The door opened, squeaking from the release of pressure. The door slid between two thick panels, their exit opening up to the vastness of space. Stephanie smiled. The light of a nearby star caused a flare in her visor. She brought her hand up to cover it. She always took a moment to soak in the view before leaving the shuttle.

Stephanie activated a small tablet on her exosuit controls. She kicked on propulsion systems. Small thruster expulsions of air pushed her from the door. Stephanie gave a quick whip to the long harness keeping her attached to *The Sterna*. She wriggled the harness, loosening the slack to give her room in the wide open galaxy. She didn't wait for Mike.

"Base, this is Tao. Beginning approach." Stephanie floated toward the portal.

The pane of reflective glass rested near the portal entrance with no support. A light swirled around it. The circular vortex emitted a silvery blue light. The light spun in a perimeter around a center point behind the black mirror. The middle of the portal entrance seemed to be nothing. It emulated no light, like a black hole. Yet the silver light surrounding it wasn't pulled inward, rather it moved around the center like the edge of a shield.

She analyzed the glass floating in front of the inexplicable portal entrance. It wasn't a traditional mirror. The reflection was darker, almost like a mineral crafted into rectangular form. A subtle shimmer of stars bounced back against the reflection. Galaxies and stars far from home, places Stephanie would never be able to explore. She'd explored thirteen planets in her time in space. She'd set foot on Earth-like planets, and floated through gaseous giants. More than most in the space exploration program. A hell of a run for a forty-two-year-old.

"See true fear of the self. Destroy the fear. Find the self," Stephanie whispered.

"What's that now?" Mike asked.

"Repeating what they said."

"What you believe they said."

"Mike, I was part of a team that deciphered the fifteen transmissions from this portal. I'd appreciate some confidence in my ability."

"But how do you know?" he asked

"How do you know how to fly?"

"Years of training, time in the field. I'm damned good at it," Mike said.

"Okay, then trust me when I say I've done the same with language," she replied.

Stephanie's tether tightened. She reached the end of the line. The tether whipped her back. The gentlest shift in momentum brought rapid alterations in direction. She fired four small bursts from her thrusters. Attached to her gloves and boots, the thrusters let her navigate her way through space without the older, bulky packs used in past years.

"*Sterna,* this is Tao. Joel, buddy, can you bring us closer?" Stephanie turned around, looking back at the ship. It rested 50 meters from her. She knew the exact distance since it was the length of her tether.

"Tao, this is *Sterna,*" Joel said. "Have to keep a minimum of 75 meters from shuttle to portal. Base orders. Spacewalk is authorized for a distance of 25 meters."

"My equipment is fine. There aren't any magnetic field disruptions or anything. You can come closer. Not every mission is a repeat of Zeta Andromeda, you know?" Stephanie said.

"Hey, we made it out of Zeta Andromeda because we maintained minimum safe distance, thank you," Joel said.

"Hard to argue with that."

Stephanie turned back toward the mineral pane. The black-like surface bounced the lights of *The Sterna* back brilliantly. She could see herself in the mineral's reflection. Against the rectangular form the reflection of her white exosuit. There had to be more to examine, and she had to get closer. "Joel, I'm going off the tether." Stephanie reached for her harness buckle.

"You're not authorized." Mike stopped behind her.

"The mission calls for the analysis of the portal and to answer any communications received. In order to do so I have to get closer and inspect any communications from that mineral pane," Stephanie said.

"I don't hear anything," Mike said.

"That's part of your problem, Mike." Stephanie released her harness. She fired her thrusters toward the pane. "You constantly believe all there is to communication is what is said."

"What the hell is the mineral pane?" he asked.

"It's that large, mirror-looking thing in front of the portal, but it's not traditional glass. It's some sort of mineral, likely unidentified elements. We should extract a sample if we can. I'm going to check."

Mike released his harness as well. "I wanna see."

"*Sterna*, please be advised, both crew are now off-tether," Stephanie said.

"Copy that, Tao. You and Captain Crawford are at 92 and 89 percent on thrusters, respectively. Plenty of time," Joel said.

"How have I expended 3 percent more?" Mike asked.

"Harder pushes on the thrust. It's why you keep having to constantly correct your course," Stephanie said.

She fired her thrusters again. Her right leg kicked out. Stephanie rotated her knee and spun her foot in a small circle. Each spin had a little pain shoot up into the ligaments of her knee, but the general motions relieved her strain as she moved toward the portal.

She still couldn't discern a thing from the center of the portal. It was black. Nothing. A sphere of shadow lived within the silver-blue light encircling it. There had to be more to it than a black hole. Otherwise Stephanie, Mike, the pane, even *The Sterna* would've been consumed.

"Besides being a mineral, what is this thing?" Mike asked.

"A gate," Stephanie said. "The ninth communication gave us these coordinates. The tenth told us to enter through their gate."

"Weren't there fifteen communications?" he asked.

"Yes. The twelfth warned us the entrance wouldn't be easy. The thirteenth and fourteenth gave us clues. 'See true fear of the self. Destroy the self. Find the self.'" Stephanie slowed her approach. She reached five meters from the portal. She could now see her facial features through the reflection. Its clarity was astounding. The reflective minerals had to be crafted. The senders of the message made this pane. Something about it had purpose. Once she knew why, she felt the portal would reveal more than the spherical darkness.

"The fifteenth?" Mike asked.

"What?" Stephanie asked.

"What was the fifteenth communication?"

"The formal invitation," she said.

Stephanie looked at the swirling silver-blue light around the portal. They weren't streams of light; there were hundreds of thousands of specs moving in a unified stream. It was a collaborative flow like a flock of migrating birds. Each spec varied its vibrancy. Small shimmers came from the infinitesimal orbs. They flickered. "That's not light," she said.

"How is that not light?" Mike asked. "It's a bright color surrounding a black space."

"We're seeing light, but those specs are small elements collaborating into a collected movement. They're emitting bioluminescence," Stephanie said. "They're signals to each other to maintain a connection. Their light signals the path, the specs behind them follow that, reach a point and emanate bioluminescence for those behind them. They're persistently showing each other the way."

"Oh my god, Mike. We've made first contact," she said.

"Those are aliens?" he asked.

"They're not likely the ones who sent the communication, but they are an alien species. They emit bioluminescence like fish and crustaceans in deep ocean ecosystems back home," she said.

Mike stared at the black, reflective surface in front of the portal. He remained in place.

"Mike, I'm talking about behind the pane. Look at the swirling mass around the portal center." Stephanie pointed at the black entrance.

Several of the specs broke away from the stream of the circular flow. They engulfed a singular point on the portal entrance, then returned to the stream.

"Did you see that? They swarmed something that came out of that entrance. They're protecting it. Whatever came out must be a food source," Stephanie said. "Joel, you're capturing this, right?"

"Hell yeah! We've just discovered biological Reciprocal Altruism in space. By protecting the portal they gain resources as a reward," Joel said.

"You should come out here and see this once we're done," she said. "You'll be able to inspect these things closer."

"Yes, please. Please," Joel said. "I'm contacting Base. Telling them the good news."

"We're not alone in the universe. It's proven now," Stephanie said. "Mike, can you believe that?"

He didn't answer.

"Mike?" Stephanie asked.

She turned around. Mike remained fixated on the pane. His fingers swiped at the dark mineral surface, scratching at the smooth black sheet.

"Mike, what are you doing?" she asked.

He lowered his hands and engaged his thrusters. The captain of the exploration mission retreated from the pane, headed for *The Sterna*.

"Captain?" Stephanie watched him retreat. "Captain Crawford, what is your status?"

"Those life forms are unverified. How do we know their intentions aren't hostile?" Mike asked.

"Sir, if you'd allow a biologist to advise: your proximity was close and they did not engage. Their size would prove problematic in attacking creatures of our size," Joel said.

"I'm falling back," Mike said.

"Sir, you can't," Stephanie radioed. She stared at the mineral pane. A subtle reverberation emanated across the dark gray layer. The pane altered its external surface. "Permission to remain on external mission."

"Permission granted," Mike said. "Knock yourself out. I'm done."

Stephanie couldn't understand how her captain perceived the pane to be a threat, yet not call the entire crew back. She kept her focus on the task at hand, understanding the pane and its correlation to the portal entrance behind it. The surface glimmered as it rippled. A small current of movement flowed from the bottom. It crawled from a small fracture line and spread out in a fanning motion up the black matter. Like the wake of a boat jetting across a lake, a single point shot upward, echoing down the entirety of the pane.

"Captain? Did it move when you stared at it?" Stephanie asked.

There was an odd silence, more than she'd ever had with the normally outspoken captain. "Yes," he replied.

As the rippling split flowed toward the top, Stephanie could see a mirror-like reflection. She could make out the wrinkles in her white exosuit, and could articulate the individual stars behind her.

The ripple moved up, passing the midway point. Her reflection changed. She still floated in space, but the reproduced image altered from the truth. Blood stained the exosuit at the knee. She reached down, clutching at her knee. She wiped at the exosuit, checking for blood. Nothing. Looking back at the mirror, her reflection had not moved. It wasn't a reflection, but a transmitted image of herself sent back to her by this mirror. This gate. She was watching a projected image. Blood seeped around the joint, soaking the leg of Stephanie's exosuit. The leg swelled. The image bouncing back at her revealed Stephanie's reflected face, stricken with fear. Her actual face was one of confusion, yet the projection played out a different version of herself.

Stephanie moved her arms to verify whether the image was a true mirror or just a fictional representation. It reflected none of her movement. The mineral pane actually fabricated a visual likeness. Stephanie couldn't understand why it showed her knee bloodied and swollen. She looked down, seeing a perfectly normal leg, yet the reflected version was a panicked Stephanie, putting pressure on the knee.

"Mike. Captain, what did you see when you looked in this pane?"

The radio remained silent. Stephanie dissected the behavior of her projected image, frenetic and scrambling to stop the bleeding. The reversed theater of her own life played in front of her.

Another ripple popped from the bottom of the pane and wriggled up. As the wave ebbed and removed the panicked version of herself, a new image reflected back at her. The image was at Base, the central command for space exploration missions. Stephanie sat in Base, complacent. Her eyes nearly shut in a fight against exhaustion. Stephanie sat at the guidance controls of her space exploration headquarters. She carelessly moved about her day. No exploration. No spacewalks. Just the mediocrity of computer-aided guidance. This surface played for Stephanie a simplistic vision of her near future. Life after this exploration ended.

Her reflection remained stagnant, not moving from the guidance desk. Stephanie hated this reflection; it was what she feared would happen after returning home. She wanted the projected image to stop. The version of herself in the projection tried to stand, but she remained at the desk. A lock kept her tethered to it by her injured knee. It was her deepest fear realized. She knew her knee was giving out and would keep her from further missions. Base would give her a task at the main headquarters for others. From there the rest of her life would be witnessing others explore areas of space she never could. She hated this projected image. Stephanie wanted space. She wanted exploration.

"Captain, what did you see?" she asked again. "I'm seeing myself, broken, unable to venture out here in a new galaxy."

The radio remained silent. Finally, Joel broke in. "I'm genuinely confused."

"This mirror." She continued, "it shows you images of yourself. It's shown me two images. The first was something I fear. The second was what people have told me to do once we return home. What they want me to be."

"You're seeing an alternate version of your own life?" Joel asked. "Those bioluminescent creatures must be doing more than protecting that portal."

Stephanie watched as her reflected version remained seated. Co-workers lined up, placing stacks of papers on her desk. She took them all, accepting the boring nature of bureaucracy. She understood the pane showed a deep fear. What she failed to understand was why.

"What did you see, Mike?" Stephanie asked one more time.

She turned from the pane, not wanting to see the office version of herself anymore. The captain remained silent over the radio.

"Captain Crawford!" she shouted.

"I stood in front of you," Mike radioed.

"That's it?"

"I stood in front of you and asked for you to be with me. I was naked and you wouldn't have me."

Stephanie turned back. The black mirror had stopped showing her images. The small flecks of light—the creatures circling the pane—moved with a calm flow around it. Behind it all was the portal to the unknown.

"Stephanie," Captain said.

"Stop," she replied. "I know you respect me to have kept boundaries between us on this expedition. I know you also have feelings for me. That doesn't mean I'm comfortable going any further into the conversation right now."

"I understand and I apologize."

Stephanie fired her thrusters. She extended one hand toward the dark gray threshold to the portal beyond. The creatures moved around the pane in the same calm pattern. They didn't come after her as she drew closer.

Her fingers stretched out toward surface. It felt like stone. The slick exterior had no give, yet moments ago it rippled like water. Stephanie pressed against the mineral, testing its strength. A crack formed where her middle finger pushed. The dark gray surface turned to silver where she applied pressure. Stephanie pushed harder. The rest of her fingers broke through the pane. The cloth on her exosuit gloves shook from a gust of gravity coming from the portal behind the pane.

She withdrew her hand. A break in the glass-like surface revealed the portal, a swirling vortex pulling to a single point of light emanated toward an unknown destination. By breaking through the pane, she could somehow see the portal differently.

The creatures circling the pane left their formation, entering through the newly formed hole. Their bodies flickered before entering, then disappeared as they thrust toward the single point at the end of the portal. They shot out flecks of light.

"They're signaling the way in for others to follow," Stephanie whispered.

A few of the creatures remained, stopping at the fracture point on the pane. They lingered, waiting for something. Stephanie inspected them closely. They had eighteen small legs, creating a circular standing base. The creatures didn't have wings, rather they had small pores all over their body. Stephanie observed one creature firing bioluminescence from one of the openings. It propelled the creature. They used gas expulsions from their pores to pilot through space. It flew toward her and landed on her glove. The ladybug-sized creature rested there. The rest of the aliens on the fractured opening followed, landing on her right arm. The suit glowed with bioluminescence creatures surrounding it.

Stephanie stared through the hole she created in the mineral pane. Beyond it was the portal, a vortex ending in a light she'd never seen. No human had ever seen it. She'd found something new to all of humanity.

"Are you guys seeing this?" she asked. She tapped the camera on her helmet.

"Every second," Joel said.

Stephanie thought she could see more detail in the light at the end of the portal. There were varied heights, different shades. It was moving. Whatever it was that waited for her was nothing humanity could've ever contemplated due to the limitations of the world they inhabited. This portal contained technology incomprehensible to the human mind.

"Make sure you keep recording," Stephanie said.

"Why?" Joel asked.

Stephanie did not answer, but engaged her thrusters. Her body flew forward, right arm extended. The creatures flew from her arm. They all fired their bioluminescence, and entered the hole in the pane. She followed them in. She crashed against the surface and it broke into thousands of pieces. Her helmet and shoulders cut through the opening, expanding it wide enough to allow her through.

Stephanie felt a force similar to, yet unlike gravity pull at her. It felt like invisible rope engulfing her body and pulled her toward the portal. The sound of the captain yelling over the radio came through, but she couldn't make him out from *The Sterna*. The signal lost clarity, turning to static.

She fixated on the point of light for stability. She had no way of knowing if a human body was capable of going through this portal, but she had to be the first. She didn't care if she became the first to die in an attempt to speak with an alien species. That was one version of the story. Another was Stephanie making it through, and experiencing what waited on the other side.

She didn't know, but as the vortex pulled her in, she saw why the point of light had so many variances. The light was a city, a floating metropolis atop an asteroid. The lights were different colors, but created with the same bioluminescence as the creatures guiding her through the portal.

Stephanie knew the pane was a test; a threshold to vet the weak and strong, to determine who could enter the portal.

"See true fear of the self. Destroy the fear. Find the self," she said.

She watched as the vortex expanded around her. At the end, she saw the floating city. Stephanie Tao headed for the unexplored. She entered the portal, knowing she was the only person in all of humanity to experience this.

WHEN I LAST SAW YOU
Julia Loving

When I last saw you I felt a certain way
You looked through me as if I had nothing to say
I watched as your eyes looked me up and down Feeling
you were uncomfortable I said, "Let's just sit
down."
The conversation was distant even though you knew my
heart's core
Even though I lost 46 pounds you probably wished I had
lost more
You see, at first I lost the weight for the love of you
But now that I know better I should not have to change for
you
In private you claim we have this loving relationship
But in public to dance with me you would always skip
But like Hughes says, "I laugh, eat well and grow strong."
And a few months from now you will be embarrassed and
ashamed because you were wrong
To have ever looked at me and said you wish I was more

THE PHOENIX
Ashley Vasquez

I never thought my whole world would be reduced to ash overnight. What high school junior did? As my childhood home burned to the ground, I looked at the pieces left over and found there wasn't much I wanted to salvage from my life. I hadn't realized how far I'd strayed from the woman I wanted to be, but as devastating as the fire was it turned out to be my salvation.

*   *   *

"Jordyn, this is your dress," my best friend, Serenity, called from the next aisle over. I waded through the sequins and taffeta of the formal section in the department store, hoping that the giggling I heard meant that Kayley and Serenity were just having fun, and not having fun at my expense. Shopping with just Serenity was hard enough, but with Kayley there I expected to be the butt of all their jokes.

Serenity and I had been friends since elementary school, but when we got to high school Serenity joined the cheerleading squad, and sometimes I got relegated to the background. Kayley was the nicest of the cheerleaders, but the look in her eyes every time I wasn't picture perfect made me cringe. The last thing I needed was her judgment, but she'd invited herself along and Serenity hardly ever said no. At least I knew she'd be brutally honest and not let me pick something the rest of the school would mock me for.

Serenity held up a dusty purple gown with just a little bit of sparkle. I smiled a little and took the gown, avoiding looking at the price tag.

"Take this one too." Kayley handed over a slinky black dress with cutouts on the sides and back. Then she turned and hefted up several others. "And these."

Examining the rainbow assortment of gowns, I barely restrained myself from rolling my eyes. I knew I could discount some of them right away. The yellow mermaid would make me look like more of a pineapple than Frenchie did in *Grease*. The aquamarine dress looked like it was built for a girl with way more bust than I had, even with the help of a pushup bra.

"You're the only one who doesn't have a dress yet." She glared pointedly down her nose at me and added, "Or a date."

Serenity twirled, holding up another dress. "I heard that Bobby Collins wants to ask you. You like Bobby, right?"

I shifted the dresses in my hands, buying myself some time. Nothing was wrong with Bobby, but there wasn't much right about him either. Being captain of the football team and the self-proclaimed school hottie didn't do anything for me. "Isn't he going out with someone? Jennifer Allen, I think?" I turned before either of them could argue. "I should try these on."

Serenity took half the stack of dresses from my arms. "I'll help." As soon as we were out of earshot, she leaned in. "Are you sure you want to do this? I thought you didn't want to go to prom."

I shrugged halfheartedly. "It's what teenage girls do, right? Mom's been talking about it for weeks. At least she's not trying to pick out my dress. Can you imagine? I'd be in puffy sleeves and lace, like she was." I claimed an open dressing room. "It could be fun. At least you'll be there. We both know you'd rather dance with me than George. Why are you even going with him?"

"What? He's not that bad. At least he hasn't taken as many hits to the head as Kayley's boyfriend. He's still got some brain cells left." She handed over the pile of dresses. "I'll be right here if you need help zipping or anything."

Locked in with a sea of taffeta and satin, I wanted to drown in the fabric and put myself out of my misery. Closer inspection of the gowns confirmed my fears. Almost all of them were far out of the budget I'd set, and those that fit my price requirements looked more like tents than dresses. I wanted to scream. Instead, I reached for the first dress on the pile. The one Serenity picked was almost my style; I put it aside to try on last.

The next dress was the black one that Kayley had thrust at me. With her pale complexion, slight frame, and white-blonde hair, I imagined she could've played a Bond girl in a dress like this. As soon as I had it on, I knew it was all wrong. The sleek edges were lumpy and the cutouts framed the rolls of back fat that I just couldn't quite get rid of.

I was about to pull it off when I heard Kayley call, "We want to see."

Grumbling, I stepped out of the fitting room and faced my firing squad.

Serenity gave me a kind smile. "It looks good." There was a slight hitch in her voice, betraying her lie.

I rolled my eyes and crossed my arms. "No, it doesn't. I look like a cow."

Kayley pursed her lips. "Oh Jordyn, you do not, but that is *not* your dress." She didn't elaborate. "Go change. We're not leaving here until you find your dress."

I went back into the dressing room and avoided looking at the daunting wall of gowns. Wishing I could rip them all into glittery confetti bits, I tugged off the black dress and let it pool at my feet. I bent to pick it up just as my phone rang.

I fumbled with my purse, not daring to make eye contact with the mirror while wearing nothing but my underwear, until I managed to get the cell out. Mom's face filled the screen and I slid my thumb across the bottom to answer. "Hi, Mom."

"Jordyn, where are you? I called the house a dozen times. I need you to start dinner."

Internally, I did a happy dance: an excuse to stop wrapping myself in sequins for the judgment of others! However, I knew my friends could hear through the door, so I curbed my excitement. "I'm at the mall, looking for a prom dress. Can't Alex do it?"

"Alex is at baseball practice. Coach says he's got a real shot at actually playing this year. I can take you shopping this weekend."

I let out an exaggerated sigh. "Fine. I'll go home."

"While dinner's cooking, start on your homework. I love you." Her last three words felt more obligatory than honest. I couldn't remember the last time she'd said those words to me and I'd actually believed her.

"Bye, Mom." I hung up and quickly tugged on my jeans and the ruffled shirt Kayley made me buy the last time we went shopping. I didn't like the way it hung on me, but Kayley raved about how good it looked, so I handed over the money. Resentment came later when I realized that my car had needed an oil change, and so I had to put in extra hours frying chicken and flipping burgers for minimum wage to pay for both.

I deserted the gowns, lifeless on their hangers, and headed out.

Kayley stuck out her lower lip in a fake pout that I knew she used to get her way with boys. "You can't leave. You don't have your dress."

I shrugged. "I'll come back when I have time. We've still got weeks before prom. I'm sure I can find something." I fidgeted with the zipper on my purse, hoping they wouldn't invite themselves along on the next try.

Kayley grumbled. "You need our help. I've seen what you pick out when you don't have us with you."

"Well, I guess it's a good thing you practically live at the mall." I forced a smile and fished out my keys. "See you at school tomorrow."

Serenity followed me toward the exit. "I can tell her I'll help you. You don't have to deal with her if you don't want to."

"No, it's fine. She's got good taste… some of the time."

She gave me a quick hug. "Okay. Call me later?"

"If I can. You know how Mom gets about me having my cellphone out. I don't get why it's such a big deal. It's not like they help pay for it."

Serenity scoffed. "They pay for Alex's, don't they?"

"Yeah, well, he's doing sports, so he doesn't have time for a job. Never mind that I do extracurricular activities too." I pulled my purse back up onto my shoulder. "I'll talk when I can."

Serenity headed back to Kayley and I hurried to my car to get home.

*   *   *

At home, I dumped my backpack on the couch and went to the fridge. Mom was anal about pre-making and freezing meals, and as I expected, there was a lasagna defrosting on the middle shelf. I pulled it out and followed the hand-written instructions to preheat the oven. I shoved the foil pan inside before it was fully preheated, not caring that Mom had told me not to do that.

I knew Mom and Dad would expect a salad and bread too, but I wouldn't have to deal with those for at least an hour. I turned on the television and pulled out my homework, starting with my favorite subject, astronomy. It wasn't a typical high school class, but my school partnered with the local community college and twice a week I got out early to go to the campus and take real college classes. I couldn't wait to graduate and take more. Astronomy was just the start. I wanted to go to space.

The front door slammed. My brother dropped his backpack and baseball gear in the entryway, then kicked off his shoes, leaving them to stink up the whole room. He flopped down next to me on the couch and picked up the remote.

The couch cushions jostled and I smudged the line I was drawing. "Dude! You messed up my star map." I yanked the remote back. "I'm watching this."

Alex rolled his eyes. "You shouldn't be doing your homework on the couch. Mom'll kill you if you get ink on the cushions again." He glanced at the TV. "How can you do your homework *and* watch TV?" He snatched the remote back and flipped it to ESPN.

I muttered under my breath, "At least I'm doing something. I'm not going to be the one flipping burgers my whole life."

"What?"

"Nothing." I picked up my stuff and moved to the kitchen island to finish my homework. "You should clean up your crap. Mom hates it when you leave it at the door."

He shrugged. "She never says anything to me."

I scowled. She didn't. I was the only one who ever got yelled at for not being neat enough. Alex's room could get quarantined for toxic sludge and she still wouldn't tell him to clean it.

After I finished my astronomy homework, I put the garlic bread in the oven. The lasagna made the house smell like an Italian restaurant — a huge improvement over my brother's socks. I still needed to do my English and history homework, but Mom and Dad would be home soon.

With a sigh, I mixed up the salad, silently throwing curses at Alex. Mom never made him help get dinner ready, even when he didn't have practice. She never said so, but I knew it was because it was "woman's work," just like the dishes, the vacuuming, and laundry. If it didn't involve a grill or a lawn mower, no one expected Alex to know how to do it.

"You could help set the table, you know."

"Coach said I should rest up for the game. I don't want to pull something." He looked over the back of the couch. "Besides, it's your night."

I rolled my eyes and grabbed plates out of the cupboard. We were supposed to alternate nights for setting the table, but somehow it was always my night.

Mom came home and got out a bottle of wine and a couple of stemmed glasses. As her hands worked the corkscrew, she watched me get the lasagna out of the oven. "Jordyn, are you putting on weight?"

I nearly dropped the hot dish. "Excuse me?"

"You should take a walk around the neighborhood after dinner. Your jeans are looking a little snug." She popped the cork before adding, "Maybe take more salad than pasta tonight."

I set the lasagna on a hot pad and pulled the bread out, dumping it onto a cutting board. "Okay, Mom."

After Dad came home and we gathered around the table, dinner conversation was dominated by Alex's chances of playing the Friday night game. I ate in sullen silence, fuming about the fact that no one bothered to ask how my day was, let alone offer a "thank you for making dinner."

"Jordyn?"

I blinked a couple of times as I looked up from my lasagna. "What?"

"Are you going to your brother's game?" Mom gave me a pointed stare.

I scowled. "I'm in the play. All weekend. You promised to come see me on Friday."

She tilted her head down in annoyance. "Your brother only has one game this week. Can't you miss one show? We'll come see you on Saturday."

I dropped my fork onto my plate with a loud clang. "If I don't go on Friday, they're going to replace me with the understudy, and I won't get to act all weekend. We don't even know if he's going to play."

"Jordyn, that is no way to talk to your mother. We'll come to the play on Saturday." Dad took a sip of his wine, which was his way of saying that the subject was closed.

I picked up my dishes. "I'm done. I have homework, so I'll be in my room."

Mom frowned. "You hardly ate anything."

I scraped my leftovers into the garbage, eyes locked on Mom the entire time. As the last bit of lasagna fell into the white plastic bag, I said, "You should be happy. If I don't eat, maybe I won't be so fat."

I threw open the dishwasher and slammed my plate and cup into it, and shoved it shut again. Grabbing my backpack, I ran from the room before she could say anything else.

My stomach rumbled as I flopped down on my bed, but I'd made my stand. I'd rather go to bed hungry than face more of my mother's judgment.

*   *   *

My alarm went off and I dragged myself from bed, trudging down the narrow hall to the bathroom to stake my claim before Alex got up. I locked the door and turned on the shower, rubbing the sleep from my eyes. As my foot was half inside the tub, I noticed my towels lying on the floor in a wet heap. I cursed Alex under my breath and pulled fresh towels from the linen closet, frowning at the fact that instead of using the soft terry cloth that I specifically picked out, I was now stuck using the old threadbare towels Dad had in college.

Shampoo bubbled in my hair when Alex pounded on the bathroom door. "Jordyn, I need the bathroom. Get out."

I kept lathering. "I'm in the shower. Use the bathroom downstairs."

"I need to shower too."

"You're going to have to wait."

The doorknob rattled and I waited for him to bust in. It wouldn't be the first time he'd forced the lock open. The rattling stopped and I quickly finished showering before he could find one of the keys.

Wrapped in two threadbare towels, I scooped up my pajamas and all the rest of the towels I could find. It was spiteful, but if I had to give up my right to a decent towel, he didn't deserve any at all.

I kicked his bedroom door as I walked past. "All yours."

I dumped the pile of terry cloth onto my bedroom floor and then opened my closet. Sometimes I thought it would just be easier to let Kayley come over and pick out all my outfits for the week. At least then I wouldn't have to agonize over what to wear every day.

Flipping back and forth through every shirt hanging in my closet, I settled on a deep purple oversized sweater and black leggings. I looked at myself in the mirror over my dresser and frowned. Even on my best day, I didn't look like I belonged in the same group as tall and slender Kayley or petite and bubbly Serenity.

I blow-dried my hair and turned on the curling iron, hoping to add a little life to what my mother called "dishwater blonde." While the curler heated, I applied mascara and bold eye-liner, trying to play up the part of my face I actually liked before covering my eyes with glasses. I ran the scalding hot curling iron through my hair.

"Jordyn, you're going to miss breakfast," Mom shouted—like she did every day—from the bottom of the stairs.

I sighed as I looked at my limp curls in the mirror. They'd have to work. Darting out the door with my backpack over my shoulder, I called, "Running late, Mom. I have rehearsal tonight, don't forget."

The door slammed behind me. I ran down the driveway to my car. It was constantly moments from falling apart, and I put more money into it than it was worth, but it was mine. I'd worked all summer to buy it and it felt like freedom.

I stopped at Serenity's house on the way to school. Serenity's mom scolded us both constantly that there was a reason the house came with a doorbell, but neither of us wanted to spend more time in that house than necessary. Her parents were in the middle of a messy separation, but sill lived together. It felt more like a war zone than a home.

Serenity jogged out, her long auburn hair swaying with each bouncy step. I envied her ability to look great wearing the simplest outfits; I could never pull off a black tank top and jeans that well. She pulled open the car door and smiled. "Hey, Jordyn."

I put the car into gear again and we rumbled down the street toward school. While I drove, Serenity drove the conversation, prattling nonstop about prom. I didn't think she even noticed my silence.

In the parking lot, Kayley met up with us. Kayley's scrutinizing eyes inspected every choice I'd made for the day. "Jor, why don't we dye your hair this weekend? I could give you highlights."

I bit my lip. I didn't love my hair color, but Kayley once came to school with fire engine red streaks, and I loathed the idea of her getting anywhere near my head with chemicals. "I'll … think about it."

She reached over and ran her fingers through my hair. "I just want you to be your prettiest."

I shifted my backpack and mumbled, "I gotta go to the library before class." I hurried off, feeling like I'd failed the Kayley inspection once again.

My first two classes of the day passed uneventfully and I filled my notebook pages with doodles of satellites, rockets, and asteroids. I knew that my doodling made me look like a bad student, but I always knew what was going on; I just didn't need notes to absorb the information.

Finally, third period rolled around. When I signed up for my class load for the year, I was under the impression that Advanced Placement meant I wouldn't be stuck in a class that didn't challenge me, but apparently I had bigger problems than feeling too smart for the material.

"Jordyn, pull your hair back. Safety procedures." Mr. Thompson tapped on the poster on the wall to punctuate his point before wandering around the room to check on the progress of the rest of the class.

I could hear Mr. Thompson talking to the boys as he circled the room. "Good job, Matthew. A little less of the acid, Bobby, but you're getting it. Keep going, Chris." He hardly stopped long enough to see what was going on in their labs.

Then he rounded back to me.

"Jordyn, you're moving a little slow on this lab. Are the instructions too hard? Do you need me to pair you with someone more advanced?"

More advanced? Was he kidding? He posted grades every week. Even though I didn't know how anyone else ranked, since the list was comprised of pseudonyms to keep our identities secret, I always took the number one place. Who could he possibly pair me with that would be more advanced? I clenched my fists under the table and said through clenched teeth, "I'm just taking my time to get it right."

"Think of it like a recipe. Maybe that would help." He leaned closer, studying everything on my table. "You could keep your space a little neater."

I stared at him, at a loss for words. My workstation was neater than any of the boys'.

"You know, Jordyn, I applaud you for taking this class. I know how hard it is for you, but next year, if you go to college, you should consider only taking science classes at the community college level. I wouldn't want them to hurt your GPA."

My lip curled into a snarl and I squeezed my hands into tighter fists, but before I could say anything else he moved on.

I finished my lab with several minutes to spare and cleared off my table, eager for the bell to ring so I could leave. Bobby Collins strutted over, goggles slung around his neck. His smile was a little crooked and his hair was intentionally mussed to look like he'd just rolled out of bed. "Hey, Jor. I hear you don't have a date yet for prom."

I sighed. "So?"

"So, how about I take you?" He jerked his head up in a half-nod.

"I —" The shrill ringing of the bell cut me off, and I grabbed my bag and darted for the door before he could ask again.

*   *   *

Kayley plopped down next to me as the cafeteria filled up. She leaned toward me and said, "Did Bobby Collins ask you out in third period? What did you say? You better have said yes! He's so cute, like one of the cutest boys in school. You totally have to go out with him."

"I haven't answered him yet."

She froze, her Diet Coke inches from her open mouth. "What? You have to go find him right now, before he asks someone else. A guy like that doesn't wait around forever."

I was tempted to ask what kind of guy he was; she talked about him like he was a prize, but I didn't see it. Before I could say anything, Kayley grabbed my hand and yanked me off of the table bench. She pulled me through the lunchroom and I did my best to not look like I was dreading the planned encounter.

"Bobby," Kayley called, pulling his attention from his friends. "Jordyn was just telling me how you asked her to prom." She batted her eyelashes and leaned forward so that even I was staring at her cleavage.

"Yeah, I thought it'd be cool. You goin' with me then, Jor?"

"Um…" I bit my lip and looked for any way to avoid answering. Kayley elbowed me and stared with pursed lips. "Yeah, okay."

He nodded. "Cool. I'll pick you up at six."

Kayley tossed her hair over her shoulder and smiled. "It was great talking to you, Bobby."

As we walked back to our usual table, I asked, "If you like him so much, why are you pressuring me to go with him?"

"What? Don't be stupid, Jordyn. I'm with Brent." She shook her head. "We have to go shopping after school."

"I can't, I have a dress rehearsal."

"Oh right, the play thing. After, then, come pick me up at my house. You have to have a dress. You're going with *Bobby Collins*."

"I'll see if I can. I've got to keep up with my homework."

"Oh, whatever. You already got into like three of your top schools. No one cares about your last semester of senior year."

I crossed my arms and scowled. "I care."

She laughed. "Whatever. Dresses. Tonight."

I picked at my lunch, not really hungry for the limp lettuce and waxy, anemic tomatoes. I glanced at Bobby, laughing with his friends and eating a greasy slice of pizza. Why did I say yes?

My eyes scanned the cafeteria until they settled on the boy I really did like. Not many people noticed Trevor Washington. He certainly didn't fit in with any of the cool groups—usually reading Tolkien and drawing pictures of dragons on the borders of his books—but he didn't hang out with the nerds or geeks either. He sat alone, nose in his book. I idly wondered if Kayley would have been so eager for me to accept the invitation to prom if it had come from Trevor instead.

*   *   *

After rehearsal, Kayley grabbed my hand and dragged me toward my car.

"I can walk on my own, you know." I tugged my hand away. "I thought I was picking you up."

"Oh, I know, but you're not getting out of dress shopping. I already called your mom. You're mine as long as it takes. All night, if we need it." She grinned as she grabbed the keys from my hand. "Your mom is so glad you have a date."

I forced a smile. I hadn't intended to tell my mother that I had a date at all, or at least not until right before he picked me up. "You're not driving. Give me my keys back."

Kayley shook her head and unlocked the car to slide into the driver's seat. "You're not doing anything except trying on dresses. Get in the car and relax."

I cringed, but climbed in and buckled my seatbelt. The argument wasn't worth my energy. From the moment Kayley put the car into gear until she shut it off, I death-gripped the edge of the seat with my eyes squeezed closed. Kayley's driving was definitely no way to relax.

Once more, I found myself surrounded by taffeta and satin. Before I could even look at the aisles of dresses, Kayley grabbed dresses at random as she pulled me toward the dressing rooms. "Try some on, I'm going to shop more." She tugged the door shut.

I shuffled through the dresses she'd grabbed, and picked the only one that was in my size. It was a two-piece dress in deep crimson. It wasn't my style, and I worried about the way the top was cut—exposing my shoulders and midsection—but I quickly changed into the dress, knowing that if I wasn't quick about it, Kayley would likely try to come in.

Standing in front of the mirror, I assessed the situation. The skirt swished a little with movement and actually did a pretty good job of hiding my lumpier areas. The beaded top sparkled under the harsh fluorescents of the dressing room, but I was surprised to see that the beads didn't make me look bulkier. Afraid to look at my shoulders or back, I opened the door and walked out tentatively.

Kayley was nowhere in sight as I stepped up to the hundred and eighty-degree mirror, twirling slightly. The racerback cut of the top actually covered the areas I dreaded seeing the most, and although it was two pieces, my midriff only showed when I moved certain ways. A wide grin spread over my face.

"No. That's too flashy for you, Jordyn. I brought some better ones."

I stepped away from the mirror and scowled at the stack of dresses in her arms. "Okay. Which one should I try first?"

Kayley hung up the pile and pulled out a simple A-line dress in a dusty blue. "This one. It's more your color, don't you think?"

I took one last longing look at myself in the fiery red dress before going back into the dressing room to try on more. After what felt like an eternity of Kayley nitpicking every detail of every dress, I settled on the least offensive choice: a navy blue, empire waist dress with straps and no sparkle. I didn't love it, and I secretly felt like it made me look like I might be five months pregnant, but Kayley gave it her stamp of approval so I let the cashier ring it up.

"Want to get dinner in the food court before we go?"

I shook my head. "I have homework." It was a feeble excuse, but my stomach was in knots and the last thing I needed was fried food.

"Boo. You're being a wet blanket."

I knew I shouldn't fall for it, but it was my senior year and she was still my friend. "Homework could wait for a little while, I guess."

Kayley grinned and linked my arm with hers. "We should also see about getting you some new underwear. You're going to prom with *Bobby Collins*."

I cringed as she dragged me toward the black and pink neon of Victoria's Secret. "He's not going to see my underwear."

Kayley pursed her lips. "You never know. It's prom."

I did the only thing that I could think to do: I pulled my phone out and pretended to answer a call. "Mom? What's up?" I waited a few seconds. "But I'm shopping with Kayley." A few seconds more. "Fine." I made a point of looking like I hung up and then shoved the phone into my pocket again. "I have to go. Mom needs me."

"Again?" Kayley stuck out her lower lip.

I extricated my arm from hers. "See you tomorrow."

*   *   *

Heat poured in through my bedroom window. The fans did nothing to cool the May air. It was too hot to sleep. I stared at the orange peel texture of the ceiling and imagined the shapes were creatures, telling their stories like hieroglyphs. My favorite was a smudge that looked sort of like a phoenix, wings spread wide in flight.

I didn't notice the smoke at first. It crept under the door like clawing fingers.

My eyes just barely closed when the alarms blared through the house. I jolted up and dropped down to the carpet, my body reacting before I could fully comprehend what was going on. I crawled over to the door but I didn't even have to touch the wooden surface to feel the heat radiating behind it. I choked on the smoke filling my room. There was no time to decide what to save. Even if I knew what I wanted, the dark grey haze was too thick.

I crawled to the window and shoved the screen out. Trembling, I gripped the edge of the window, taking in a deep breath of fresh air as smoke poured out over my head. The grass seemed too far from my second story bedroom, but I didn't know what else to do. I hoisted myself over the ledge and jumped, eyes squeezed shut.

I landed hard. A crack echoed through my ears as pain radiated up from my leg. Tears welled up in my eyes as I saw my left ankle was bent at the wrong angle. Somehow, I pushed through the pain to haul myself to the sidewalk.

Sirens wailed down the street and I leaned against the front tire of my car to watch my home burn. Everything I owned was in my room except for a superhero t-shirt Kayley hated and the grungy pair of pajama pants I wore to bed.

Mom and Dad ran out the front door, but I couldn't see Alex anywhere. I gingerly hoisted myself up and limped toward the fire truck. I tapped one of the firemen on the shoulder.

He glanced over his shoulder halfheartedly before turning back to what he was doing. "Miss, I need you to stay back."

"I think my brother's still in there. I haven't seen him. His name's Alex..."

He turned to really examine me. I was leaning heavily on my right foot; my left barely touched the asphalt. "Is this your house?"

I nodded.

"I'm going to get a paramedic to look you over. What's your name?"

"Jordyn." I winced a little as I shifted my weight. "I'll be okay. Please find my brother."

"You said his name was Alex?"

I nodded again.

He reached up and clutched the mic on his shoulder. "I need a paramedic team over here at the engine. Teenage girl, possible sprain or break in her left ankle. Anyone see a boy named Alex anywhere?"

I leaned against the fire truck, trying to take any weight off my ankle. I kept scanning the growing crowd but I couldn't see Alex. He was a jerk, but I didn't want him to die in a fire.

Two EMTs in matching dark blue uniforms came over, one carrying a red first aid bag. "Miss, can you walk?"

I shrugged. "It hurts."

One of them wrapped his arm around my waist and pulled me against him. I gingerly leaned into him, afraid to put too much weight on him.

"We're going to get you over to our ambulance, okay?" He started moving forward, and I hopped along with him. Every painful step I worried that I was too heavy, that he would drop me or that I would fall, but they successfully helped me into the back of the truck.

As he checked my ankle, the other one said, "So, was jumping out the window you trying to emulate the superhero on your t-shirt?"

I coughed. "No, it was the only way out."

He smiled a little. "Just trying to break the tension. Who's your favorite hero?"

We talked about different comic book characters while my ankle got wrapped in an ace bandage. My lungs burned, and the more we talked, the more I coughed. When they were done with my ankle, the superhero fan patted me on the knee. "You just sit tight. We need to get you x-rayed and make sure nothing's broken."

"Will you let me know if they found my brother?"

"Of course. I'll be back to check on you soon." He gave me a plastic mask connected to an oxygen tank and helped get it situated over my nose and mouth.

As they left, I laid down on the gurney, staring at the medical instruments and cabinets of supplies in the ambulance. I don't know how long I waited, but I must have fallen asleep because the next thing I knew, I was in a hospital bed. My injured ankle sat on a stack of pillows.

"Oh, you're awake." The bright, bubbly voice seemed like a harsh contrast to the muted colors of the décor, and it cut through the quiet of the room like an ax.

A girl with a mass of black curls and sepia brown skin and warm eyes was propped up on a bed next to mine. "Hi."

"I haven't had a roommate in a while. What's your name? I'm Izabis, but you can call me Izzy."

"Jordyn." There was a privacy curtain between our beds, but it wasn't pulled. "What are you in here for?" She seemed too lively, too happy to be in a hospital.

She pulled back the covers and I cringed when I saw that she had a stump where her right calf and shin should be. The stark white bandages stood out against her thigh. "They cut it off with a saw."

I jerked my gaze back to her face, trying not to stare at the missing limb. "Why?"

"I have a dirt bike and I was trying a new trick. The back wheel hit a rock, I went flying, and the bike followed. I'm lucky it didn't pin more than just my leg. I might be able to ride again one day."

I stared, in shock. The way she said it, it sounded as mundane as tripping or missing a step and falling down. "You lost your leg."

She shrugged. "I don't see it as a loss. Life's too short to be upset about a missing leg. I get to be bionic now."

I smiled despite everything.

She leaned over and raised an eyebrow. "What're you in here for?"

I bit my lip. I didn't have a cool story like hers. "I broke my ankle, I think, jumping out of my bedroom window. The house was on fire."

"That is so… badass." She checked the clock on the wall and sighed. "I should probably warn you that my brother's going to stop by before he goes to school, so he might be here soon."

I quickly confirmed that I was still wearing my t-shirt. I didn't want to meet anyone's brother wearing a hospital gown. "That's fine. I'm surprised no one's come in to check on me."

"Oh, your mom was in earlier but you were asleep, so she left again."

A knock at the door drew our attention. It swung open and I immediately looked away. What was Trevor doing here? I pulled my covers up a little higher and ran my fingers through my hair. I didn't want to know what I looked like after fleeing my house.

"Hey, Iz. How's the foot?" He walked right past me and sat on the edge of Izzy's bed. "Looks like you got a roomie. Who's the new girl?"

I smiled a little. "Hi, Trevor. I didn't know you had a sister."

His eyes grew wide and he shifted, turning to face me. "Jordyn? What are you doing in here?"

Izzy grinned. "She jumped out of a burning building. We're going to start our own adrenaline junkies club."

"I only did it because it was the only way out. It's definitely not something I want to repeat."

"Still, you've got Izzy's respect. That's worth a lot." He patted his sister's thigh, just above her bandage. "Considering how much of a thrill seeker she is, I have no doubt your jump was as cool as she thinks it is."

I could feel my cheeks getting warm. "What about you? Is Izzy the only adrenaline junkie in your family?"

He laughed and shook his head. "The only adventures I need are the ones written in books. I'm more than happy to let Iz do the crazy stunts."

"I bear that burden with a grin on my face because life's too short, and stunts are too much fun."

Trevor leaned over and kissed her cheek, brushing a wild curl out of his sister's eyes. "Just try not to lose any more limbs. You don't have that many left."

"Trust me—that's one thing I never need to do again, but up until that bike pinned me it looked really cool."

He shook his head, smiling. "I've got to get to school. Promise me you won't do anything stupid."

She stuck out her tongue playfully. "I make no promises."

I watched him walk toward the door. I knew so little about him; I hadn't even realized he had siblings. As he turned and smiled at me, I felt a flutter in my stomach. "Jordyn, do you want me to bring your homework when I come back?"

"That'd be great. I don't want to fall behind."

He stepped closer to me again, but stopped just shy of my bed. "Maybe I should get your cell number? Just in case they discharge you."

I frowned. "It was… in my room."

"Well, then I'll just have to trust the pipsqueak over there to let me know if you get freed."

"I don't even know where I'd go."

He reached out and touched the blanket over my right foot. "I'll hope you're still here when I get back then."

Once he was gone, Izzy said, "You're that Jordyn?"

"What do you mean, *that* Jordyn?"

She smiled. "Oh yeah, you're her."

Just then a nurse came in wearing a bright set of scrubs in a cartoon character print. "I see both my patients are awake. How are we feeling?"

"Well, see, it's the damnedest thing, but I definitely remember having two legs when I walked in here," Izzy joked.

I snickered. "I'd say we're both doing just fine, considering."

Izzy grinned. "We just had a visitor, in fact." Her tone was laced with mirth.

"Izabis, you know you're not supposed to have visitors outside of regular visiting hours." The nurse's stern tone would've had me cowering, but Izzy just laughed.

"Oh, come on. It was only Trevor. It's not like it was one of my many, many adoring fans." She leaned forward a little and gestured for the nurse to come closer. Izzy loudly whispered, "But he might be Jordyn's adoring fan. I'd keep an eye on her. She seems like trouble."

I feigned a shocked gasp, pressing my hand to my chest. "Me? I'm completely innocent."

The nurse shook her head. "Great. I've got two troublemakers on my hands." She checked Izzy over and then came over to check on me. "How are you doing? You took a pretty nasty fall."

I thought for a minute about how to answer. Physically, I felt drained and achy. Everything I knew, everything I ever had was gone. "I feel... okay, I guess." My head felt a little swimmy and I thought I should be in a lot more pain.

She smiled. "If you're joking around with Izzy, you must not be feeling too bad." She ran through the care I was getting and then showed me how to use the remote on my bed to call for her if I needed anything. She told me that my brother was in the Intensive Care Unit suffering from severe burns, but that they thought he'd make it through. I breathed a sigh of relief. Alex was alive.

Before she left, she offered to send my parents in. "No, that's okay. They should stay with the kid who needs them. I'll be all right here."

The nurse left Izzy and me alone again, and I sat in quiet reflection for a moment before I said, "How do you do that?"

"Do what?"

I bit my lip. "Just say whatever's on your mind. Joke around with anyone. Aren't you afraid you'll get in trouble?"

"What are they going to do to me?" She shrugged. "Trevor coming by to check up on me doesn't hurt anyone. Besides, life's too short to let someone else dictate how I should live."

I leaned back, thinking about what she'd said. "You just speak your mind? No matter what?"

"Yeah. Why not? I'm happier doing what I want, being who I want to be, than I would ever be following someone else's rules. Even with a missing leg, I'd rather be on my bike than anywhere else in the world. Hasn't anything ever made you feel that way?"

"No."

"Nothing?"

"Well..." I glanced over at her, thinking. "You won't think it's stupid?"

"Jordyn, my favorite thing to do cost me a limb. Do you really think anything you say could be stupider than that?"

Softly, I murmured, "There was this prom dress…"

"A dress? Tell me about it! Who's taking you to prom? Do you have a date?" Her voice grew more excited with each question.

"It's not the dress I bought, but I guess the one I *did* buy sort of went up in flames." I let out a hysterical laugh, shaking my head. "It was hideous." After I caught my breath, I told her about the red dress I'd tried on, the one that I'd considered actually buying before Kayley talked me out of it. Then I told her about Bobby Collins and how he'd asked me out in AP chemistry class. Before I could stop myself, I told her about how my chemistry teacher didn't think I was smart enough to take science classes, but I really wanted to be an astronaut, and about how not even my parents believed I could do it.

Izzy was quiet for a long time and then she said in a determined voice, "It's a good thing you met me."

I smiled at her. "I guess so."

Izzy looked over, her eyes heavy. It was the first I really thought about the fact that she was in the hospital missing a leg. "I think I'm going to sleep a little while. Trevor left a couple books, if you want something to read."

I nodded. "That would be good."

She handed over The Lord of the Rings trilogy. "I couldn't get into them, but maybe you can." She pulled her covers up and rolled over. Before I even really had time to say anything else, she was snoring softly.

I picked up the first book of the trilogy. I'd never been much for reading fantasy. Trevor had handwritten notes and sketches in the margins and I quickly became immersed not only in Middle Earth, but in the flourishes added by Trevor's small, neat penmanship.

"Iz passed the books on to you, huh?"

I gasped and looked up, surprised to find Trevor's warm, dark brown eyes looking at me. "When did you get here?"

He smiled. "Just now. I brought your homework." He dropped his messenger bag next to my feet.

"Is it okay that I'm reading your book?" I could feel my cheeks turning red.

He nodded. "At least someone's getting use out of them. I tried to talk Iz into reading them, but she doesn't do well with sitting still. Even when she's bedridden." He pulled out books for my classes. "Do you mind if I stick around a while? I usually hang out until dinner time."

"Sure." I looked down at the book again. "You've got some serious talent. Your drawings really make the story come to life."

He looked like he was embarrassed and handed over my schoolwork. I thought his cheeks were flushed, but his dark skin made it hard to tell. "Sometimes I just get inspired when I'm reading…"

Our fingers touched as I took my books and I drew a sharp breath. "Well, I like them." I dropped my homework onto the nightstand and looked over at him again. "How was school today?"

"All anyone could talk about was your house burning down. Someone started a rumor that you started the fire, but Serenity shut that down pretty quick." He sat on the edge of the bed and picked up the novel propped on my knee. He scanned the page briefly and said with a grin, "You're at a good part."

I laughed. "It's better than staring at the walls. I have to say, I've never read a book like this, and I don't think I'd be surviving it without your notes and drawings."

He fidgeted a little with his shirt hem. "If you ever want to talk about it, I've read those books a dozen times."

"Why don't we talk for a while? Unless you're in a hurry to get into your homework."

He smiled softly and put his own books away. "I'd like that."

*　　　　　*　　　　　*

Once the doctors were sure that my ankle was the extent of my injuries, they released me with a walking cast. Mom and Dad had secured a room at an extended stay hotel while they sorted out insurance. Mom didn't want me going back to school or work right away, but not even Trevor's books could keep me from feeling like I was going crazy, trapped in a small suite with my parents.

Each day, when they left for work, I headed back to the hospital, glad that at least the freedom of my car wasn't gone. I visited Alex every morning, sitting next to his bedside. He still hadn't woken up. Part of me feared he never would.

When I couldn't take staring at my brother's bandages any longer, I would take the elevator down to the floor Izzy was on. I spent my afternoons talking and laughing with Trevor and Izzy, feeling more like myself than I had in a long time. Serenity came by for dinner most nights, and my parents were actually being supportive and helpful. The best times were spent with Trevor. He made my days bearable.

"Jordyn, are you listening to me?"

I blinked a couple times and focused on my mother again. "I'm sorry. It's the pain medications I'm on. My mind wanders." I was stretched out on the stiff hotel couch, my foot propped up on pillows.

"I brought your mail from the post office."

"Great. Thanks, Mom." I took the stack of envelopes from her. I didn't usually care about mail, but a few of the parcels were college acceptances, and those I was interested in.

She sighed and sat next to me. "Jordyn, you've only got a few months left at home with us. Can you try a little harder to be a part of this family? Your brother's still in the ICU and you haven't even gone to visit him."

"Uh, if you haven't noticed, getting around hasn't been the easiest for me. And for your information, I have gone to see him. I sit with him at least an hour every day. Not that you'd know it, because you leave me alone every day. You don't care about me, as long as dinner's on the table and dishes get done."

She recoiled like I'd just slapped her. "Jordyn, where is this coming from?"

I scoffed. "Are you kidding me? This past week is the first time I haven't felt like an imposter in my own life. I'm so over being treated like I've got to do everything around the house because Alex is a boy and on some stupid sports team. I missed my play, but you haven't once asked how I'm feeling. I can't wait until I can pack up my belongings and get as far from you people as I can. Of course, I don't own anything anymore, so that makes it easier." I slid off the couch and crossed my arms over my chest, crumpling my mail under my arm. "You know what the funny thing is, Mom? If the house hadn't burned down, I might never have had the guts to say that to you." The corners of my mouth turned up and I said with a bit of a laugh, "If I can convince him to, I'm going to prom with the school nerd. I really like him."

Mom stood up and reached for my hand. "Jordyn, if you were feeling this way, why didn't you say something sooner?"

"You never listen. You make promises, and then as soon as Alex wants something, what I want gets dropped. Even now, I get looked at like I'm this huge inconvenience. I jumped out of my window because I couldn't get out of my room any other way, but you don't even see the courage it took to do that. All you see is that inconveniently got hurt." I limped across the room, still trying to get used to my walking cast.

Mom's cheeks were tearstained, but I couldn't talk to her anymore. I hobbled down the hall to the elevator, needing to get away and drove to the one place I knew Mom wouldn't find me.

Izzy listened to me rant about my mother until I was out of breath, and then she grinned. "How do you feel?"

I laughed. "Really good. I'll pay for it later, but for once I told my mother how I really felt."

She held out her phone. "Keep it up and give Trevor a call."

I took the phone and bit my lip. "Do you really think he'll say yes?"

She pursed her lips and stared at me pointedly.

"Okay, okay. I'll send him a text." I stared at the screen, nervous. I had never even considered asking a guy out before.

"Jordyn?"

"It doesn't feel right to text him. I'll ask him when he comes by after school."

Izzy frowned. "You'd better."

I sat on the chair next to the window, wondering if Trevor would really go to prom with me. To distract myself from what I intended to do, I pulled the mail out of my purse. The envelope on the top was open, and I would've been angry if I weren't shaking with nerves about the return address. It was a big parcel, not like the flimsy one-page form letters that declined admittance. I almost screamed in excitement. "Izzy, I got in." I held up the welcome packet with the University of Maryland logo emblazoned on the front. "I'm going to be an astronaut."

Izzy grinned. "Don't let anyone tell you otherwise."

I read the acceptance letter and was surprised to see mom's handwriting across the top. It was simple, but it meant more to me than I realized: *Congratulations, Jordyn! You're going to do great.*

*   *   *

Life almost felt normal by the time I donned my prom dress. Better, even. Mom had started asking for help instead of just assuming I would. Alex had woken up, but was still at the hospital, fighting an infection from his burns. More than just the house had to be rebuilt, but I thought just maybe we'd end up on a stronger foundation.

Serenity styled my hair and did my makeup, and when I stood up to look at myself in the bathroom mirror of my hotel room, I gasped. The girl looking back at me was beautiful.

"Jordyn, who picked out this dress?" Serenity ran her hand over the satiny crimson skirt.

I smiled and twirled a little. "I did."

"Well, you look gorgeous. Red's really your color." She pinned a red jeweled barrette into my hair and said, "I think Trevor's in the living room, waiting for you."

I walked over to the bedroom door, more confident now on my cast. I strode down the hall, followed closely by Serenity in her emerald green dress, and grinned as Trevor rose from the couch, a white rose corsage held in his trembling hands.

"Jordyn, you look…"

My cheeks flushed.

Mom said, "Okay, let's just get a few pictures before you go."

Trevor carefully slid the corsage onto my wrist and wrapped his arm around my waist, supporting my weight so that I didn't have to lean too heavily on the boot. Serenity grabbed her boyfriend's hand and they stood next to Trevor and me as Mom took a few posed shots.

"Okay, enough. I want to actually try to dance before my foot hurts too much." I hugged Mom gently, and Trevor took my hand and led me out of the suite to the elevator.

"Are you ready for this?"

I grinned at him. "Let's go to prom."

I Am Beautiful Pledge

I will love and respect my body. I will love myself for

who I am and treat my body with kindness.

I am beautiful inside and out.

I am beautiful just the way I am!

Signed,

*X*_____

RESOURCES

If you have questions about body image, self-esteem or eating disorders and would like to learn more, you may find the following resources helpful:

<u>**National Eating Disorders Association (NEDA)**</u>
at nationaleatingdisorders.org
Supports individuals and families affected by eating disorders, and serves as a catalyst for prevention, cures and access to quality care. Their site contains resources for anyone needing more information or support.
They also have a helpline:
<u>**NEDA toll free, confidential helpline**</u> **at 1-800-931-2237**

Worried you or someone you love might need help? Take this free, anonymous online self-assessment:

<u>**My Body Screening**</u> **at mybodyscreening.org**
<u>**Proud2BMe**</u> **at proud2bme.org**
An online community created by and for teens. They cover everything from fashion and beauty to news, culture, and entertainment—all with the goal of promoting positive body image and encouraging healthy attitudes about food and weight.
<u>**Project Heal**</u> **at theprojectheal.org**
Offers a scholarship program to fund inpatient, residential and outpatient treatment for eating disorder sufferers who want to recover but do not have the financial means to do so.

See Beautiful at seebeautiful.com

A movement that helps girls and women see the beauty they inherently possess instead of supporting the definition of beauty that pop culture would like us to think we have to live up to.

Life Vest Inside at lifevestinside.com

Strives to empower and unite the world with kindness. LVI is geared towards spreading kindness, empowering people and building self worth.

Endangered Bodies at endangeredbodies.org

An international local-global initiative. They challenge all those merchants of body hatred who turn girls and women against their own bodies.

MissHeard Media at missheardmedia.com

MissHeard aims to break the mold of traditional teen media by focusing on girl-centered and girl-created content to foster empowered, girl-positive communities.

The Body Positive at thebodypositive.org

About radical self-love, inhabiting our unique beauty, and reconnecting to the voice of wisdom.

Miss Fit Girls at missfitgirls.org

A nurturing after school program that encourages adolescent girls to explore their authentic selves, to become more mindful and to strengthen their confidence through yoga-based activities and community partnerships.

Perfect As U Are at perfectasuare.com

Clothing helps girls boost their confidence and embrace their beauty through continuous affirmation of their undeniable and immeasurable value.

For even more information, check out our resource page: **realizeyourbeauty.org/resources**

MEET THE AUTHORS
AND POETS

Beverly Coutts lives in the Denver area with her husband and three hooligan dogs. She has her Masters in Economics and currently works as a budget analyst for the State, which she loves more than any normal person ought to. She is obsessed with science fiction and fantasy, and has been writing as a hobby since she was in elementary school. When she isn't reading or writing, she's usually playing video games or collecting more random hobbies.

Jason Evans always wanted to be a writer, he just didn't know it. He grew up in Pasadena, California, in the 1980s, with his mother and sister, Ann. His wasted youth was interrupted by graduating from the University of California, Santa Barbara, with degrees in History & Renaissance studies, in 1996. He earned teaching credentials from Cal-State Los Angeles sometime later.

After meeting with the love of his life, the fetching Mrs. Evans, they married and moved to Denver, where Jason worked as a teacher for ten years and earned a graduate degree in History at UC Denver. Jason is currently blogging for Pikespeakwriters.blogspot.com, while seeking a publisher for his first two books. He resides in Denver with his wife.

Thomas A. Fowler has written movies, plays, short stories and books. While he sticks primarily to science fiction, he dabbles elsewhere. He was nominated for Best Original Screenplay at the Paranoia Horror Film Festival. Another movie he wrote, "The Code: Legend of the Gamers," is available on IMDb and screened at film festivals. His short stories have been published by RuneWright Publishing and Story of the Month Club. He holds an MBA in Marketing from Regis University and uses that to work as a Producer & Content Creator in advertising in Denver, Colorado. Somewhere between writing and advertising, he tries to be a loving husband and responsible father.

Jessica Lauren Gabarron has been enchanted with the written word from the moment she first learned how to write a complete sentence in school. Jessica has lived in many states in the USA, and most recently, has called Colorado her home for the last thirteen years. During the day, she works with the loan department in a bank, but she spends her nights dabbling in more fun hobbies and crafts. When her fingers aren't busy flying over the keys of her laptop, Jessica is also a licensed massage therapist. Jessica can be found in several places on the internet, including the Sidekicks anthology, Adventures in Zookeeping anthology, and Domesticated Velociraptors anthology, all listed on Amazon. Her blog, Over the Moon, is found at www.jlgabarron.com. To keep up with current events in J. L. Gabarron's life, including conventions in and around Denver, Colorado, follow her on Facebook at Facebook.com/JLGabarron and Twitter, @JLGabarron13 and @13Kingdoms.

Julia Loving is an avid reader, lover and teacher of Africana history, literature and culture. As a teacher of Library and Information Science for more than 20 years, she shares her appreciation of books and history with youngsters in New York City. In her spare time, Julia Loving is a lindy hop/swing dance enthusiast who dances competitively and socially. She recently started a blog entitled "Big Girls Lindy Hop Too" (biggirlslindyhoptoo.blogspot.com). This is a safe space online for plus size Lindy hoppers to voice their opinions, share experiences and showcase their skill set. Her motto is LIVE, LOVE, LAUGH AND DANCE FREE FROM STIGMA.